TALES FROM THE DEN

DARK FICTION VOLUME 1

JESSICA RANEY

JAE MAZER

LDM INDUSTRIES

He's mad that trusts in the tameness of a wolf…

— William Shakespeare, King Lear

CONTENTS

PREFACE

What is this, you ask? Tales from what den? Where? Who? Why?

Well, first you should meet us. Jess and Jae. We met at Comicpalooza in Houston many moons ago, and a fast friendship was formed. Now the best of friends, we do everything together. Notably, in this context, we write. Every Thursday evening, you can find us at our Denny's, writing and chatting and critiquing... basically plotting world dominance.

Often, we enter writing contests, and prompt each other through them. After our umpteenth contest and joint writing project, we decided we had accumulated quite the collection of various stories in multiple formats. Thus was born the idea of a collection to showcase us, our relationship, and our growth.

Tales from the Den is a compilation of longer short stories, flash fiction, micro fiction, and screenplays. Many of these are products of a contest called NYC Midnight in which competitors are given writing prompts and a specified amount of time to generate a story. For example, in the flash fiction contest, we were given a genre, a character, and an object, and had 48 hours to compose a 1500 word story. In this past year, participating in these contests alongside each other, we have made it through more rounds than we ever did while tackling NYC Midnight alone.

The interesting thing for you as readers is to get a taste of the very distinct styles in this book. Though the stories sometimes have overlapping themes or penchant for the horrible, the voices are very different. You will get a unique insight in to each mind, as terrifying and unsettling as that might be.

So enjoy this book as a product born from friendship and love, and the never ending quest to become better, smarter, stronger writers. And this will be the first of many of these collections, so watch for us. We are unstoppable.

THE LESSON

Her dress was new. Well, new to her, anyway, a hand-me-down from a cousin, light blue, dotted with little white embroidered flowers. The fabric was thin in places and some of the little flowers had unraveled, but once it was washed and pressed carefully, the dress had new life. She twirled in a circle to make the skirt flow out and smiled at the way the little white flowers twinkled in the morning sun. Her mother had warned her about vanity and pride and that morning her mother had given her an extra lesson about modesty. She didn't understand. The dress was so pretty, and she never got new things. If it was wrong to like the dress, then why did she have the dress? There was an extra lesson for her in not asking impertinent questions.

When the lessons were done, and everyone dressed in the nicest clothes they owned, they walked together into town. Her father walked in front, then her brothers, then her mother. She walked last, always. She didn't mind. Most of the time, she kept her head down, but sometimes, she would look up and see the sunlight glittering off the new green leaves or a little bird flittering from branch to branch, singing his Spring song. Once or twice, she dared a twirl, to see the dress move and the little flowers dance. Afterwards, she looked up carefully at her mother and father. If they saw, she would have more lessons later. Her mother's head was bent, and her father was walking steadily, setting the pace for them, his head straight and his eyes on the path, not on her.

It was an important day, the most important of the year and everyone had come. Families that lived farther out than hers had come; some must have begun walking days before to make it on time. Everyone looked tired and slightly rumpled from their long journey. The women nodded at their husbands then carried their baskets filled with family lunches and suppers to the rough picnic shelter. The boys mingled and talked quietly amongst themselves, while the girls lined up next to the shelter and said nothing.

They had all had many lessons.

They were supposed to keep their heads bowed

and pray. She never did. The things she was supposed to ask for, humility, modesty--obedience, she didn't want, and she wasn't sure anyone was listening anyway--despite repeated lessons to the contrary. This was the first Spring Gathering she had been allowed to attend, fully. She attended worship services, of course, twice a week, but this was an event. In past years, parents ushered the small children out and they spent the night in someone's home, where they read scripture and sang songs until their families collected them the next day. Her parents said the Spring Gathering was special. She wondered what made it special. Nobody would tell her. Her brothers, who normally liked to tease her with all sorts of tall tales about everything were sedate and quiet about this.

She was hot. They were standing in direct sunlight and while the morning had been cool, the sun was at full strength now and its bright rays and the layers of clothing were making the girls sweat. Mercifully, the worship bell rang. Seven long, slow chimes signaled everyone to assemble and begin. The small children were collected and taken by a group of women. Everyone else filed into the worship area. It was different from the normal area. Set back into the forest a quarter of a mile from the main church, the land was cleared. There were roughly hewn wooden benches and a rudimentary stage and altar. There were poles and lanterns surrounding the entire area, but none of that seemed at all remarkable to her. What was remarkable was the area to the left of the pulpit, a perfect circle of dead grass. It wasn't burned or charred, just dead. Brittle and gray, the circle stood in stark contrast to the tender, green grass that grew thick and luscious all around it.

Her father led them to a bench, and they sat down when he did. It was no different than any other service that she had ever been to. The main difference was the silence. There wasn't the usual friendly hum of conversation that preceded a normal service. Nobody said anything. In fact, nobody moved. No fidgeting, no shuffling in seats, everyone sat still and stared directly ahead. Her brothers both looked pale and nauseated, as if they were both about to throw up. Her mother was sweaty and kept her head bowed, her lips moving in silent prayer. Her father sat there sternly as he stared at the altar.

She didn't know how long the silence lasted but it was finally broken when the Pastor climbed on the stage and took his place in the pulpit. He instructed everyone to stand for the invocation, which was the longest one she had ever heard. The clearing was in full sun and it was stifling hot with no breeze. It was difficult to stand still but nobody dared move, not even to fan themselves.

When the Pastor was finished, he motioned for some of the fathers to help him and they brought out a big copper kettle. It was steaming hot. The men used thick woolen mittens to handle it and when they placed it on a tripod in front of the altar, she could see the wisps of vapor and waves of heat. The pastor gave another long-winded blessing over the kettle, then he dipped a ladle in and extracted some of the liquid. He poured some out on to the spot of dead, brown grass and he drank a ladle full himself. He coughed and his face reddened, but he didn't do anything else remarkable. He motioned for the fathers to bring their families forward. Each father obliged. They led their family to the kettle and each took the ladle and made every member of their family drink. She could tell that several did not want to drink. They looked afraid, their faces pained and locked in a grimace even before the ladle touched their lips. But they had no choice in the matter. The fathers forced everyone to drink. When her own father led them to the kettle, her mother swallowed her portion without any complaint and went back to praying. Her older brother did the same and her middle brother sniffled a bit, but he drank.

She was unprepared for the smell of the liquid when her father put the ladle to her lips. The steaming brown liquid smelled like the outhouse in the middle of summer and burning hair. She wrinkled her nose and took a step backward, but her father's eyes flew wide and his mouth got the angry white ring around it. He grabbed her and pulled her closer, then grabbed her chin and poured the liquid down her throat. She doubled over and coughed and sputtered. It was the most vile, bitter, foul tasting thing she had ever put in her mouth. She thought she might throw up, but her father grabbed her chin and held her mouth closed. The sick came up, but had no place to go, so she swallowed it down and he dragged her back to their seats.

Once every person in the clearing drank the liquid, the men put the kettle away. The Pastor began to read scripture. After a while, people in the crowd began to shout at him, their words were gibberish. He ignored anything except the book in his hand and kept reading. His voice started out as a dull drone, but as time went on, he got louder and more animated. His face turned beet red and he sweated profusely, his white shirt front soaked through with brown stains. Everyone in the audience was sweating too. Her own blue dress was completely drenched, and her hair stuck to her head. The world was spinning, and she could no longer hold in the sick. She threw up all over her dress front and she wasn't the only one. All the children had vomited on themselves, some of the older teens too. Most of the adults looked sick, but only a few of them had. Her father and mother were drenched in sweat and pale looking but they looked otherwise well enough. Her mother had raised her hands to the sky and was swaying back and forth, speaking in gibberish and her father's eyes were flashing as he growled and shouted encouragement to the Pastor.

The Pastor screamed and she couldn't understand anything he said. He'd gone on for hours and it was dusk now. All the colors were dark orange and vibrant, like nothing she had ever seen before. If she hadn't been so sick and confused, she might have said the world looked beautiful. But it was still so hot, and everything smelled like vomit and body odor, the smells and heat hit her in never ending waves and cramps gripped her stomach. She soiled herself as had everyone else in the clearing. The whole place stank of vomit and urine. Some of the children had fallen over. They twitched every so often and she didn't think they were dead, but that was the only indication that any of them were alive. Her older brother joined a group of men who were tearing at themselves and pounding the area around the pulpit as the Pastor spoke. She had never seen him act that way before. He was normally quiet and docile but now he was a wild thing, beating his fists bloody against the rough wood.

Someone started a chant. It was nonsense to her, but soon almost everyone picked it up, including her parents. She couldn't get it and she stood silent as everyone else sang. After a bit, a father screamed a blood curdling yell, not a fearful sound, but one full of anger and rage and they would grab someone and pull them to the circle of dead grass. She watched her Uncle yell and grab her cousin Ava. Ava screamed and vomited, terrified. Soon the circle of dead grass was almost surrounded by struggling, screaming pairs. Her mother was frantically praying and beating her hands against the bench. Her middle brother was doing the same and they cried out when her father raised his hands to the sky and gave the loudest, most rage-filled yell of them all.

Her father grabbed her. Her instinct was to run, and she tried, but he was too strong. He easily pulled her to the edge of the circle. She kicked and clawed at him, bit down hard into his arm and he slapped her so hard one of her teeth came loose. The Pastor stepped into the circle. As he made his way around the circle, he told stories of each person. He detailed how bad they were and how they had sinned. One boy was too soft and feminine. One girl, not soft enough. Some were lazy. Some didn't listen well. When he stopped in front of her, his list was long. Prideful. Disobedient. Questioning. The Pastor spat those words out as if they were the same vile, brown liquid they had drunk earlier. His face was angry red and white rage spit formed at the corners of his mouth as he enumerated everyone's sins.

Finally, he turned to the middle of the circle and began to ask for help. She couldn't tell exactly who he was asking to help, but everyone else seemed to know because they began chanting a name. The name wouldn't stick in her head, so she couldn't say it even if she wanted to, all she could hear was the steading chanting of the crowd. The Pastor seemed satisfied. He turned back around to them and began running around the circle. He stopped in front of each pair again and raised his hands, letting the crowd scream for each one. They screamed for her each time he held his hands above her, her father loudest of all, but they screamed loudest for a tall red-haired boy, her oldest brother's age, seventeen or so. They found him with books. Words not in the Scriptures. Old ones.

More fathers came, and they helped drag the boy to the middle of the dead grass. He was crying and fighting them, but like her, he had vomited and was so sick and weak, that he couldn't put up much fight. The Pastor prayed over him and what words she could make out sounded like an offering. The Pastor fell to the ground, beating the dead grass, imploring someone or something to help the boy. The crowd resumed the chants and they added in pounding of their own.

Through the gibberish and the drumming, she

could hear something else. Something very faint at first, as if it were far away and as it got closer, it got louder. The ground shook slightly, but just as the rumble got louder, the tremors got stronger as well, until finally, the whole dead circle of grass was churning and vibrating.

The Pastor stepped out of the circle as did the men holding the boy. He tried to run, but he tripped and fell flat. A thin black root emerged from the ground and hooked his ankle. The boy pulled his foot free and stood up, but as soon as he tried to run, another oily black tendril snaked out of the ground and caught him. A few more attempts netted the same result, as if the root were mocking him. The crowd was still chanting and pounding and as they did, a big mound of earth in the center of the circle appeared. A thick black trunk began to push its way out of the dirt, slowly at first, but then it gained momentum as it seemed to feed off the energy of the crowd. It rose up, at least fifteen feet from the earth, dripping putrid black oil. She could smell it and it smelled worse than the liquid in the kettle, as if every dead thing in the world had combined their rot and decay.

The boy was sitting on the ground. A few of the tendrils held him there but she didn't think he would move anyway. He was staring at the trunk, and he was listening. She could hear it too, a whisper and while she couldn't make out the words, she could hear the quiet hatred in them. The boy was sobbing as the voice kept whispering the hatful words that only he could understand.

Black, putrid tendrils pushed their way out of the ground. They slithered toward the boy and wrapped themselves around his torso. Slowly, they pulled him to the trunk and pushed him up into the air. One tendril wrapped around his left arm and positioned it above his head. Another did the same thing with his right arm. The tendrils snaked around the trunk and plunged into the boy's wrists. He screamed, and the crowd cheered and drummed louder. He screamed again when the oily tendrils pierced his feet. The tendrils that had encircled his torso released and he was supported only by the wounds in his wrists and feet. The crowd cheered and danced as the boy writhed. She wanted to look away, but her father saw, and he held her head steady. She tried closing her eyes, but it made her dizzy, so she had no choice but to watch the boy's misery and to listen to the malicious whispers and the hate-filled chanting of the crowd.

It took the boy all night to die. It finally happed as dawn was peeking over the treetops and when he died, the crowd fell over, exhausted and spent. She passed out too and when she woke up, the trunk and the boy were gone. The circle of grass remained, but the ground was undisturbed. It was as it had been before, yellow-gray, dry, dead grass.

She was filthy. Covered in vomit and her other body fluids, her pretty, light blue dress with the delicate white embroidered flowers was ruined. Her father burned it, along with everyone else's soiled clothes after they had washed. Some people ate, the adults, the ones who had seen it before. She couldn't. She wasn't sure she could ever eat again. After somber goodbyes and quiet well wishes, the families started home.

As she walked behind her mother, she kept her head down and tried not to vomit again. Her head throbbed, and her stomach was still cramped up. She glanced up once at the tree tops and smiled at the light glinting off the fresh green leaves of the canopy but her smiled faded and she bowed her head again when she heard the voice begin to whisper, and this time, she could understand every word.

CREATED BY YOU

"How do you answer to the charges?"

The air was hot and heavy in the chamber and damp with the stench of day-old oatmeal and boiled blood. Ophelia scrunched her nose and looked around the room.

Blood cascaded down the obsidian walls-a macabre waterfall. Sconces crafted from skulls of all species acted as holders for the only light in the room: flames lit on wicks of spun human hair and wax. The audience groaned and chattered, jawless maws with tongues clicking off sharpened teeth. They were all anxious for torture, pain, punishment.

"Girl." Though he hadn't yelled, his voice boomed through the immense chamber, a baritone drum in a well. "I asked you a question, girl."

Ophelia regarded him with a narrowing of her eyes. He was large—many times the size of a tall, thick human—with skin of scarlet, horns of black bone, and a forked tongue that licked out at her, anxious, hungry. He sat perched upon a throne of mummified corpses shriveled and shrouded in blood-soaked gauze, tied together by some manner of intestine.

"I heard your question," Ophelia said, voice strong and sure. "And I don't."

Like a pack of rabid chimpanzees, the crowd erupted into squeals and yelps, excited by her disobedience.

"You don't what?" he asked, his throbbing black orbs for eyes growing larger each time he spoke.

"I don't answer to the charges, these or any other. I answer to no one and nothing but myself."

Another explosion from the crowd, screams and laughter, and a spray of blood from a ghoul who'd gotten so excited he chomped the neck of the changeling that stood next to him.

"Is that so?" The Dark One stroked his long, braided, black goatee, and the lice within came to life, hopping and crawling over his pocked face. He licked them all away with a swipe of his meaty tongue.

"That is fact," she said, crossing her arms over her chest.

A warm, soft paw rested on her shoulder, drawing her attention away from the throne.

"It's okay, Garmr," Ophelia whispered to her companion. She reached out and Garmr bent in half, low enough for her to scratch his ears.

"Dinnae do this," Garmr growled, bloody drool dripping from his black lips.

"It is done."

"Not yet."

"In my mind it is, so that's that."

Garmr puffed his cheeks and blew out a huff of air, defeated. Dipping his head, he took a step back and dropped to one knee, taking his place as sentry behind Ophelia.

"My old hound." The Dark One laughed, the bones of his throne crackling under his immense weight. "Attached to this one? After such a short time. Pity you'll be licking the flesh from her bones soon."

Garmr said nothing, but Ophelia could feel him tense behind her.

"You try to scare me," Ophelia said, hands on her hips.

"Scare you?" the Dark One said, head cocked.

"Yes, you mean to intimidate me. But you will not succeed. I will not be bullied and badgered, nor will I give you my fear. I have nothing to fear but myself."

The sound of his tongue clucking against the roof

of his mouth reverberated through the chamber, bouncing down from the endless ceiling and landing upon her with force.

"Intimidate you," he said, pausing to hold his side while he laughed. This time, the masses cowered, backing away. His laughter either meant satisfaction or fiery rage. Usually the latter.

"Do your worst," she challenged, a sting in her tone.

Silence. The crowd scattered like rats, more interested in self-preservation than entertainment. The Dark One leaned forward, hefting his great mass off the throne and clop, clop, clopping on cloven hooves down the many stairs, his robe of blackened human flesh trailing behind him. When he reached Ophelia, rather than bending to look her in the eye, he grabbed her by the jaw and lifted her to his face.

His breath, moist and reeking of curdled milk and spoiled meat, misted onto her face as he spoke.

"My worst is horrors you can't imagine."

Ophelia clenched her hands into fists, determined to hold strong.

You wanted this. Remember. Stay strong.

"*My* worst is horrors *you* can't imagine."

When she spoke his words back at him, his sloped, massive brown furled, darkening his entire face.

Then came the pain.

Nose to nose, he stared into her eyes, his gaze burrowing deep into her brain like a tick. He rifled around in there, shifting meat and consciousness, violating her every tissue, every blood vessel and vein, every thought. He was in her, feeling her, tasting her, devouring every cell and emotion and memory. And it burned, a fire so hot it burned white as the stars, melting her organs and shattering her bones to dust. Her eyes exploded, boiling jelly rolling down her face like globs of coagulated blood, searing the tender, freckled skin on her face.

Then her feet touched the ground, and the pain was gone.

She opened her eyes.

"Ah," he said, his tail swishing behind him, rippling his cloak. "I see."

Frantically, her hands found her face and searched her body, seeking wounds from the assault, but found herself unscathed. The pain was but a quiet echo in her memory.

"What did you do?" she said, her voice a nervous quaver.

He leaned in again, close to her ear, and whispered, his tongue flicking her lobe as he spoke. "If it's hell you want, then hell you shall have."

The walls of the chamber shook as laughter exploded from his belly. Boom, boom, boom went his hooves as he thundered back up the steps to take his perch on the throne.

"I have come to the decision," he said as he wiped a tear of humour from his pus-encrusted eyes, "that for your crimes, Ophelia Delaceur, you will be sentenced to an eternity in hell."

Satisfied, Ophelia sat on the edge of the palace wall, looking down over the hellscape below. Meandering rivers of blood and tears snaked through forests of bone and bile. Hideous animal hybrids loped around, taking chunks out of each other as they passed. The birds cried as they flapped through the air, wings of everlasting fire scorching their feathered breasts.

"I can do this," Ophelia said.

Garmr shook his head. "You know not the ways of the beast."

"I will suffer, I know."

"You cannot imagine."

"Doesn't matter. Can't be worse than…"

A dead fish. That's what she saw in her little broth-er's expression as she tightened her grasp around his tiny throat, even after his heart had beat its last. That look of surprise, of panic, of heartbreak. He had trusted her. With every ounce of his being, he placed his trust in her hands. And those hands had taken it so easily.

"It *can* be worse," Garmr said. "And it will."

The heat tingled Ophelia's skin and dried her mouth, her tongue a thick, obtrusive piece of swollen, sticky meat.

"I can handle it," she said, swishing some spit around her mouth and wiping the sweat dripping into her eyes.

Garmr's fur heaved as he sighed deep from the marrow of his bones, a resignation.

"Don't be sad for me, friend." Ophelia tucked her slender hand into his massive paw and rested her head against his muscular stomach. "I will find peace here."

With a clench of his stomach muscles, Garmr's body heaved as he unleashed a great howl to the red moon above. The howl was punctuated by a few mournful whimpers as he rested his snout on the top of Ophelia's head. She closed her eyes as his hot, rancid drool dribbled down her face.

"I am sad for you," Garmr whispered. "You do not know."

"Does anyone?" Ophelia pulled back and looked into his empty, bloodied eye sockets. "Anyone you usher here for their judgement, do they ever know?"

Garmr's jaw snapped shut, his mouth a tight,

jagged line. He turned his head to look over the cliff into the rotting abyss.

"Seriously, Garmr. Do they? Or do they just live their evil in the moment, commit mortal crimes for instant gratification, only in fear of legal repercussions?" Ophelia huffed and crossed her arms. "Who really considers the afterwards?"

Garmr shrugged. "The spiritual."

"All bullshit. They don't know. They don't even consider this side of what lies beyond. In reality—the smells, the feeling…" in the distance, a mewling human, crying through their torture and anguish, "… the sounds of suffering."

His massive wolf head turned to face her once again. "You did," he said quietly, under his breath. "And you chose suffering."

A knot formed in Ophelia's throat. She turned away from her companion and looked at her feet, bloodied and ragged from traversing the hellscape. "Yes. I thought about this. I thought about a fate worse than death, the pain of a thousand wounds, the sadness of a thousand losses." Her eyes traced his skeletal body, scrapes of bloody fur hanging from splintered bones, until she reached his eye orifices again. "All that pain has nothing on mine."

It played like a film on a reel, flickering in her

mind, out of control. All the deaths, her hands, the tools.

Her very first. Sammy. Her golden retriever with the little purple bone tag on his collar. She'd kept that collar. A trophy.

Her parents, drugged at dinner and burned in their sleep, her hand holding the match that would destroy her home and the remainder of her family.

A foster parent, a wide bloody smile opened across his throat.

Chummy, the classroom hamster, filleted on the teacher's desk.

The janitor, eyes wide and vacant, the heavy rock in her hand dripping with blood. And his hair, scalped neat and clean, resting on her own blonde curls…

"I am not a good person, Garmr." Beyond her control, her body convulsed as sobs overtook her breathing. "And I would only get worse. I've watched those shows about all those people—Manson, Bundy, Dahmer."

The fauna of Hades cackled and screeched in crescendo with her confession. It made her teeth rattle in her head and her skin crawl with the feet of a thousand millipedes.

"I deserve a fate worse than death," she said through wracking sobs. "Do you know how old I am, Garmr?"

His voice was low and sad. "Fifteen."

"Fifteen, Garmr. Fifteen. I had a whole lifetime to keep…"

A calm fell over Ophelia, a relief and realization of her position. "No. He cannot create pain for me worse than I did for myself."

All those eyes, her victims, looking at her, wondering why, pleading, begging her to stop, asking her why they'd been chosen and why she'd become the monster she had…

Garmr knew. And it was his turn to cry, silent tears dripping of mangey fur, slipping on her skin and searing through to the bone like acid. Ophelia winced at the pain but did not pull her arm away.

"Yes, this is fine," she said, a soft smile stretching her pink lips. "My punishment will be relief."

Huffing and wheezing, her steed reared its head, shaking Ophelia back in her saddle.

"Your journey will be long, my dear," the Dark One said, towering above her and pointing out over the black horizon. "Traverse my lands to your finality."

Garmr steadied the massive black stallion with a

lead made of braided intestine. Garmr glowered at the Dark One, his teeth bared.

"Do not begrudge me, Hell Host. It is she who wanted this."

"She did not know what she asked for."

"Well, she'll certainly know now, won't she?"

Laughter, raucous and taunting, vibrated the land beneath their feet. In an instant, the Dark One was gone, but his laughter remained.

"I'm sorry, M'Lady," Garmr said, slicking the hair away from his eye sockets. "We must go now."

Ophelia beamed. Atop her stallion, twenty hands high, she looked over the land as a Queen, certain of her fate.

And so the final trek began. The stallion's hooves crunched on the road made of crushed bone, grinding the bigger bits to dust. In the ditches, the damned watched this micro parade of fate, whooping and hollering as they passed. More than once, Ophelia was struck in the face by all manner of substances—animal parts, feces, globs of semen. But none of it bothered her. Her eyes were set forward, her lips locked in tight satisfaction.

"You see this as punishment," Garmr said. "You feel it redeems you."

Ophelia shook her head. "I am beyond redemption. I was damned before I ever took my first life."

The masses of other evildoers spit and hissed at her as she passed, a baptism of evil.

"You hope for punishment. Hurt and humiliation as contrition."

Ophelia did not answer. Though she knew she was where she belonged, and doomed to suffer unimaginable horrors, she also knew not what she hoped to gain.

Maybe the wolf is right. Perhaps I seek justice for my victims.

They walked. At times Ophelia would dig her heels into the stallion's side, urging him to a canter, but Garmr slowed them to a saunter before they could pick up any speed.

"Do not be in a hurry, young Ophelia. You think you know, but you do not want what awaits you at the end of our journey."

Lips pursed and brow scrunched, Ophelia contemplated the end. "Will I be raped? Sodomized?"

Garmr did not answer. One step after another, he led the horse out of the city limits and into the dark, dark woods. Above them, buzzards with heads of rats sat high in the treetops, the branches buckling from their weight. They gargled a melancholy song that brought unexpected tears to Ophelia's eyes.

"I imagine the creatures will gnaw the flesh from my bones and suck the juice from my body."

Again, Garmr said nothing, just kept walking.

The woods were horrible, rancid and pitch black, the tops of the trees curling like fingers, reaching down and yanking out clumps of Ophelia's long, curly hair. She screamed when the forest thickened, the flora surrounding her and vining over her skin like snakes, tearing away all her clothes and ripping out great chunks of her hair, scalp included.

Soon the forest passed, giving way to a seemingly endless desert with sand as sharp as glass and hot as fire. The stallion paid no mind; his feet were solid obsidian bones and all the flesh on his legs had burned and rotted off long ago.

"He has made this journey many times," Garmr said, nodding to the steed.

"Like me, he is unfazed," Ophelia said with pride.

"You must be scared. The unknown, the forth-coming pain and anguish."

Ophelia searched down to the depths of her soul, in all the hidden nooks and crevices where fear might hide. She imagined a great many things, from illness to pain, car accidents to aggressive cancer, to torture at the hands of someone like herself.

"No. Nothing can bother me now."

In the distance it appeared, on the hazy horizon, spires sprouting from the red sand like hands from a grave.

"There!" Ophelia shouted.

Garmr growled, a low, wet rumble deep in his chest. "You fool."

Paying no mind to Garmr's despair, Ophelia dug her heels into the stallion's sides. This time, Garmr made no attempt to slow them.

The stallion sped from a trot to a canter, then to a gallop, a plume of chalky red sand erupting behind them as they thundered across the desert. Ophelia broke her gaze from the structure ahead to look down at the ground whizzing by. It was not a desert, but hills and piles of bodies, dead but somehow still alive, caught in a state of decomposition that had turned them to sand. They still pained, though, their expressions full of terror as their faces were smashed by the impact of the massive black hooves.

Ophelia wanted to see no more of that. The building was close now, towering above, casting shadows across the land like bony fingers reaching for her, calling her. A heat pulsing up her leg drew her attention back to the sand.

"Garmr, what is happening?"

The stallion slowed down until he came to a complete stop. His legs had been ground down to nubs barely two centimeters long, and his belly touched the corpse sands as he struggled to move forward.

"He is done, m'lady," Garmr said. "We will need to go by foot."

Ophelia jumped down into the sand, feeling the squirm of lips and lashes against her bare feet. "No matter," she said, looking ahead. "We are just about there.

They walked. Ophelia tried to ignore the feeling of the dead sand caressing her skin, screaming faces nipping at her inner thighs and labia as the sand swallowed her to the inner thigh. It reminded her of when she lived in the north, trudging through the deep, fresh snow in the fields behind the schoolyard. She remembered Tatiana, her best friend, unconscious in the snow, her pretty freckled face smashed in by the gore-covered rock in Ophelia's own hand. How pretty that blood had been, blooming in the virgin snow like a blossoming red rose.

"I am so glad I am here," Ophelia said, taking Garmr's paw in her hand and pulling him onwards.

They were close now. She could smell the building and the food cooking inside, hear the people milling about. Whatever it was it waited for her, anxious for her imminent arrival. As she got within a stone's throw of the house of her fate, the ground beneath her shifted, sandy death morphing to yellowed grass, air shifting from hot and dry to chilly and humid. She squeezed Garmr's paw for comfort but found only her own flesh.

"Garmr?"

Looking behind, to the side, all around, Ophelia found her companion had gone, leaving her alone with her final fate. She said to the wind, "thank you, my friend."

But what is this? Where am I?

The grass was spotted with ant hills, those tiny red bastards that left welts that would itch and burn for days. With each step she took, the grass spread, revealing a yard scattered with old rusted out bikes and broken toys. Poplar trees sprouted out of the ground here and there, and birds fell from the skies, taking rest in the trees or yanking worms from the soil.

A wind chime sang in the distance, a tiny, out-of-tune melody, haunting, familiar…

A few more steps, and the looming structure before her crumpled into the grass, contorting and shrinking until it was but one story high, long and rectangular, ugly and bland.

No.

Another few steps, and a dog started barking. On the little porch of the mobile home sat a dog, Heinz '57, bone-shaped tag jingling at its neck.

NO.

Even if she had wanted to stop, which she did, she could not. Her feet were not hers anymore, and they had decided to carry her forward, up the steps of the trailer and into the world inside. *Her* world, just as it had been several years before.

Her mother sat in her chair by the window reading a cozy mystery. Her father was at the table rolling cigarettes.

"Ophelia!" her mother said through cherry red lips that gleamed in the light. "Glad you're home. Dinner's in the oven."

Ophelia's feet kept going, through the living room and down the hall to her bedroom, the room she'd shared with her brother until she choked the innocent life from his body.

But there he was, living and breathing, playing with matchbox cars on the floor, running them up and down a ramp he had constructed out of old cardboard boxes.

"Opi!" He leapt up from his play and threw his arms around her. She felt his heart pounding against her as he embraced her with every muscle in his body. When he pulled away, a scream caught in her throat.

It was her brother, but something was with him. *In* him. His eyes were solid black, his teeth sharp and rotten. His mouth was wider than it should have been, and his skin rippled when he spoke.

"I told you," he said, his voice not his own but the Dark One's instead. "You will suffer. Here. In your hell."

"I can change things," Ophelia said, tears pouring down her cheeks. "It'll be different this time. I won't do those bad things. I'll be a good person."

That laugh again, throaty and deafening, exploding out of her brother's tiny body. "No, child. You will do the same things, feel the same shame and sickness. Over and over. It will accumulate on your soul, worse every time."

Her brother stepped forward and pressed his lips on hers, breathing his rank breath of rotten meat and copper into her mouth. "Forever, Ophelia, a hell created by you."

Another laugh, this one shaking the walls.

"You are an artist of hell, Ophelia. Couldn't have done it better myself."

A blink, and her brother was sitting on the floor, playing with his cars like he had never gotten up in the first place. He looked at Ophelia, his big blue eyes beaming with love, his voice tiny chimes filled with joy. "Play with me, Opi!"

Through the open window, beyond the sounds of the squirrels and birds chattering in her yard, Ophelia could hear the mournful howls of her last friend, Garmr, and the deep belly brays of the Dark One's laughter, forever mocking her.

HIGHER LEARNING

"I wish I owned the Mona Lisa," Randy Dobbins said in a bored, sleepy tone as he reclined on the genuine Tuscan leather sofa, flipping through the recently added shows on Netflix and staring blankly at the seventy-inch ultra-high definition flat-screen television.

"You're not even trying with these wishes anymore," the demon said. "Why don't you just wish them and let me move on?"

Randy Dobbins replied. "Why would you want to move on?"

"Randy, I've been in this business for over six thousand years. I've harvested human souls and granted wishes all over this earth. One guy in Newfoundland wanted cheese shoes. A lady in

Munich asked to have the ability to understand the language of corn. If they wanted to sell their souls for those idiotic things, hey, whatever. But you, Randy, you are special. You make ME wish for finality."

A gigantic photo of Randy dressed in a starched white Gi with a black belt posed in Tiger-Crane style hung on the wall. It was a result of Randy's third wish, which was preceded by his second wish—to have two more wishes—which was preceded by his first wish: to wish always successfully for more wishes.

The dojo was empty. While it was the most well-known in the world—Randy had wished it so—he hadn't wished for any skills, nor did he have any students. "Just hang the painting there." He pointed to spot near the larger picture.

"I'm not your interior decorator. You want it hung, wish it, or do it yourself."

Randy never looked away from the episode of Cops he was watching. "Okay. I wish for two more wishes. Also, I wish you would hang the Mona Lisa where I asked you to hang it."

The demon screamed and punched a hole in the drywall, then spoke an incantation and the Mona Lisa appeared in the spot that Randy specified.

A tall, leggy blonde wearing a Dallas Cowboys cheerleader uniform stalked in and slammed a platter down on the coffee table next to Randy. "I made you pizza rolls," she said with disgust.

Randy popped one into his mouth and looked at the blonde critically. "I wish she was nicer," Randy said.

"You know I can't affect people like that," the demon said. "Maybe you should wish yourself better, Randy. This place is a dojo, a place for learning. You aren't learning anything."

"I wish for two more wishes," Randy said with a mouthful of pizza rolls, "And I wish for a nicer girlfriend."

The blonde disappeared in a puff of yellow Sulphur-smelling smoke. A short brunette with glasses and a few extra pounds came into the room with a platter of taquitos and a two-liter of Mountain Dew.

"I made you some snacks, baby," the girl said as she set the food down. She sat on the sofa next to him and tidied up his mess. "Oh, I love this episode of Cops," she said.

"Ugh, no way," Randy yelled as he sat up and recoiled from her touch as if he'd been burned. "I didn't mean uglier. I just wanted the hot one to be nicer to me." He glared at the demon. "I wish for the hot one back."

The demon rolled his eyes. "Fine."

The brunette looked confused but disappeared in a

plume of foul-smelling smoke. The disgruntled blonde returned. She slapped a handful of Slim Jims down on the table and stalked back out of the room, giving Randy the finger as she left. Before the demon could rejoice in the fact that Randy only had one more wish, Randy shoved a taquito in his mouth and wished for two more wishes.

The demon screamed.

It went on like that for the rest of the day. Randy wished for a wolf. He wished for a monster truck. He wished he alone knew the ending of A Game of Thrones. He fed the wolf pizza rolls and when the wolf got sick and crapped in the corner of the dojo, he wished for the demon to clean it up without using magic. After every wish, he remembered to wish for two more wishes.

The demon glared at him. In six thousand years, he had never felt a more vehement hatred for a human being than he felt for Randy Dobbins. Suddenly, he realized where he was—a place of learning—and realized that while Randy was never going to learn anything, he himself had learned something, even after all these years of wish-demoning. He smiled as a plan formed.

"Say, Randy," he said as he leaned against the official prop Han Solo Frozen in Carbonite that Randy had wished for last Thursday, "I have a proposition for you."

"No thanks," Randy said. He was intently watching his own personal cut of The Last Jedi.

"Just hear me out," the demon said.

Randy shrugged.

"I will grant you unlimited wishes, no more having to remember to wish for two more, if your next wish demonstrates that you have learned anything."

Randy stared thoughtfully for a moment. "You're really whiny and boring," Randy said. He went back to watching TV. "I wish I could just grant wishes myself."

The demon smiled. "Done."

Randy Dobbins had been an immortal wish-demon for only fifteen minutes and yet, he already wished for finality.

The apartment smelled strongly of cat urine and Wolf's Brand Chili. The dumpy middle-aged woman dressed in yoga pants and a pink sweatshirt adorned with glitter and kittens cried into her handkerchief and sniffed as she watched the big flat screen TV. "I wish that there were unlimited episodes of Dr. Quinn, Medicine Woman."

The demon stood behind her, laughing, as he whispered in her ear. Her face brightened, as if she'd just had an epiphany. "Also, I wish for two more wishes," she said.

The demon pounded the floor as he laughed, sending several cats running.

Randy Dobbins, rookie wish-demon, screamed.

SHE GREW WINGS

Chaos rained down from the sky, a downpour of fire and rocks and pain.

"What do you choose?"

Raya looked around at the destruction, far as her vision could reach. Homes burning, mothers huddled over children, protecting them from the onslaught.

Having nothing to lose, no family, no home, no love, Raya had no fear but the anticipation of pain. She did not know what to choose as the world stared into the face of its end.

"Raya, what do you choose?"

It was horrid, the lanky, skeletal creature before her, crooked and rotting, black as the night. It balanced on its haunches, too tall to stand straight and still look her in the eye. It was Death, and it was foul.

"I do not know," Raya said, her voice barely a whisper.

"You do not choose freedom? Safety?"

Others had. Some were clever, choosing to transport to another realm, a dimension far away from this one. But they went alone, to arrive to the unknown, to the nothing. Some chose to change themselves, to make skin of steel, or encase themselves in impenetrable bubbles. But they would stay that way forever, after all was lost and rebuilt again.

Cries echoed across the valley, the mewls of those in pain, in need, of want of their lives.

"You cannot save them, foolish chil'. The world will be rebuilt on the backs of the strong, of the worthy. You were chosen because of your strength, your independence."

"It's horrible," Raya said, the cries of the suffering reverberating in her skull.

"As it should be," Death sneered.

They were dying. All of them. Fat tears rolled down scalded cheeks, tiny hands clasped by bigger ones, lips pressed against cheeks and foreheads. Despite flaws and follies, humanity had heart. It was good.

It came to her, a wisp of a thought seeping through the wall of suffering.

"I choose wings."

Death was still.

Death stared.

Then Death laughed.

"Wings?"

"Yes, wings."

"You cannot rise above the barrage of the end."

"I want them powerful, indestructible, and as wide as the oceans."

"You hope they will carry you far, eh?"

"I do."

"As you wish, you fool."

And Raya grew wings.

A snap of a taloned hand, and Death was gone, replaced by a searing pain up Raya's spine. With creaks and cracks, her body contorted, her flesh tearing and blood spilling onto the ground as her bones reformed and muscles grew. Her scream tore through the air as the wings sprouted, stretching and growing until they were, indeed, as wide as the oceans combined.

It was the most glorious stretch Raya had ever experienced. She spread her wings, spanning the invincible feathers as wide as they could reach, brushing mountain tops and kissing the clouds. The pain was excruciating, but she did not cry out. Hot rock and fire stormed down upon the wings, but they were strong. And though she could feel it, every burning ember shooting pain through her body, the wings could not be breached.

The silence soothed the pain. The cries had stopped, the pain ceased, as the people below the shelter of Raya's wings had relief from the storm.

Their cheers doused her pain.

And joy bubbled in her belly, as she heard the anguished lament of Death in the distance, bested by wings that would not fly.

BEST SERVED COLD

FADE IN:

EXT. MUSEUM-NIGHT

Rain pours from the mouth of a gargoyle on the ancient building's facade onto the pavement in an arc.

DR. HENRY GARDNER, late 40's. Classically handsome with an arrogant gait walks briskly through the rain. He's dressed in a long raincoat, a fedora, and he carries a large black umbrella.

. . .

He sidesteps the water pouring from the gargoyle's mouth automatically, as if he's done it a thousand other times.

INT. MUSEUM-NIGHT

Gardner enters the building. He takes off his raincoat and hat. He places them on a bench in the foyer. Gardner's clothes are well tailored and expensive. He straightens them without stopping his motion and smooths his hair back.

Gardner strides down the hallway confidently. His expensive shoes rap rhythmically on the polished parquet floors.

His face is sour looking, and he is angry. He enters the gallery and stops.

A woman, **DR. KATHERINE FELLOWS**, is sitting on a bench in the middle of the gallery. She is tall, blond, mid-40's. Beautiful. Her clothes mirror Gardner's. Feminine men's wear, expertly tailored and expensive looking. She is studying a large Renaissance painting of a Pieta.

Gardner looks confused for a second. He recognizes her.

GARDNER

Kate?

KATHERINE

Hello, Henry.

He looks around the gallery. They are alone.

Katherine smiles at him.

KATHERINE

You're surprised to see me.

.   .   .

GARDNER

Well... frankly, yes.

Katherine begins to walk around the room. She stops in front of a sculpture, a grotesque that is the same style as the gargoyles outside the building. She motions to it.

KATHERINE

This doesn't really fit the theme of this gallery and it's the wrong period all together.

Gardner shakes off his confusion and replaces it with indignation at her observation.

GARDNER

This grotesque was designed by the same architect that designed this building. It matches the period of all the work in this gallery. I curated it myself.

Katherine smiles at him and laughs at his ire as she begins to walk around the room.

. . .

GARDNER

What are you doing here Kate?

She turns and faces him as she stands in front of the large Pieta painting. She folds her hands in front of her.

KATHERINE

One of these paintings is a forgery.

Gardner's face reddens. He is agitated.

GARDNER

Impossible.

KATHERINE

It's an exceptionally good fake. Just like the man who commissioned it and placed it in this gallery.

GARDNER

You don't know what you're talking about.

KATHERINE

Henry, I, of all people, am uniquely qualified to speak about the well-concealed forgery that is you.

Gardner stands off against her.

GARDNER

Is this about us?

KATHERINE

This is about five million dollars.

GARDNER

We've moved on.

KATHERINE

Yes. Yes, we have. I recovered after you stole my work. It only cost me a few years of my life. You moved onward and upward.

. . .

She gestures to the museum.

GARDNER
What do you want, Kate?

KATHERINE
You will receive a text that will provide an account number. If you fail to make the transfer within one minute of the text, evidence of your forgery will be sent to every news agency in the city as well as to all the members of the museum board.

He scoffs at her and smiles condescendingly.

GARDNER
This is far more than you have ever proven capable of.

KATHERINE
Well, twenty years is a long time for self-

improvement.

Gardner's phone chimes, indicating he has a text message. He pulls it from his inside jacket pocket and looks at it incredulously. She was telling the truth.

He calms himself and his momentary panic is replaced with his customary arrogance.

GARDNER

I have nothing to hide. I'm well- respected. An authority.

Katherine shrugs and sits down on the bench.

Gardner begins to sweat. He knows that the small portrait of the Madonna and Child opposite the huge painting of the Pieta is a forgery. He commissioned it.

Gardner pulls up his phone and taps the screen. He transfers the money.

. . .

Katherine nods approvingly. She stands up and crosses to him. She looks at his face. She's looking for something in it, but she's not seeing it. She isn't surprised by that.

Gardner looks at her. His face is red, and he is angry.

GARDNER

You have a little bit of money. I still have everything. Your dream job. The reputation. That money likely won't last you until menopause.

Katherine continues to smile. She doesn't acknowledge his anger at all.

KATHERINE

You're going to get another text. Text back "yes" and the evidence against you will be given to you.

His phone beeps. She wasn't lying. He answers yes to

the text.

His phone chimes again and his email icon appears. He clicks a link which takes him to an encrypted file share site.

It has all the evidence against him. He has the option to permanently delete. He does it immediately. He looks at Katherine triumphantly.

GARDNER

Enjoy your money while you can.

Katherine nods as she pats him on the shoulder.

KATHERINE

I've done quite well for myself. My work is nearly impossible to detect. You have to really get a good cross section and that's destructive. Nobody wants to do that, go to those lengths. Frankly, they don't really want to know the truth.

. . .

She moves past him and pauses in the doorway. She motions to the pieces in the room.

KATHERINE

These are all forgeries. Every single one. Have been since day one. You couldn't spot them. You never could.

Gardner looks frantically around the room. He has built his reputation on this gallery.

A tiny flare of light, intensely bright fires start on the corner of all the paintings. The smoke sets off the fire suppression in the room.

KATHERINE

Predictable, as always Henry. You didn't delete any evidence. You emailed it to the Museum Board and the Times, as well as the incriminating transaction. Oh, and they'll definitely see the problem with these works on cross section now.

.   .   .

Gardner is dumbstruck, staring at her and the ruined gallery. His ruined life.

Katherine salutes him. She walks out, leaving him standing in the room as the dust from the fire suppression settles.

EXT. Museum-NIGHT

Katherine walks out of the museum wearing Gardner's trench coat and fedora. She sidesteps the spout of the gargoyle as if she's walked the path a thousand times. She has.

Sirens and lights whirl around her as firemen respond to the call at the museum.

Katherine smiles and walks confidently away from the noise and light, into the shadows of the night.

FADE OUT.

HENRY'S A DICK

F ADE IN:

INT. ANNE AND STUART'S HOUSE/LIVING ROOM-DAY

ANNE is standing at the window, watching the driveway. There is a for sale sign on the lawn. STUART is sitting on the couch, head in his hands.

ANNE
I have a good feeling about this one.

. . .

STUART

Four different realtors, Anne. Is this one a magician? Did you find her on Hogwarts.com?

Anne glares at Stuart, then looks out the window.

ANNE

She comes highly recommended.

STUART

You know what I highly recommend? Hiring a marksman.

A sedan pulls in the driveway. PRICILLA steps out of the car. She is obese with large white hair, thick green glasses, and is wearing a gaudy brown dress covered in rhinestones.

ANNE

She's here.

. . .

STUART

Does she look like she can sell a house?

ANNE

She looks...

Pricilla pauses to tug on her dress, which is stuck in her ass.

ANNE (CONT.)

... like a bedazzled fart.

Stuart joins Anne at the window.

STUART

Spectacular

Anne opens the door before Pricilla rings the bell.

. . .

PRICILLA

Well I'll be tickled fuchsia!

Pricilla kisses both Stuart and Anne on the cheek.

PRICILLA

Aren't the two of you just the cutest! Two lil' biscuits, I do say!

ANNE

Thank you for seeing us on such short notice. It's been hard-

PRICILLA

(while marching past Anne and Stuart)
No need to bore me with details I already have, sugar pie. I read your file, so quit your dilly-dallyin' and let's get down to business.

CUT TO:

. . .

INT. ANNE AND STUARTS HOUSE/KITCHEN-DAY

Anne, Stuart, and Pricilla are sitting at the island bar drinking coffee.

PRICILLA

I must say I'm baffled. I cannot fathom why this place won't sell. It's gorgeous, location is good, you've lowered your price...

Pricilla tilts her glasses to the end of her nose and looks at Stuart and Anne.

PRICILLA (CONT.)

All right. Spill the beans.

Anne and Stuart hesitate.

PRICILLA

Come on, now. I haven't the time-

. . .

ANNE AND STUART
(in unison)
Henry's a dick.

Pricilla says nothing for a moment, then bursts out laughing.

PRICILLA
Oh my stars! Yes, children are a might spirited at times. Can the little darlin' be shuffled off to a Mee Maw or Paw Paw while the house is on the market?

STUART
We don't have any children.

Pricilla furls her brow.

PRICILLA
Pets can be boarded.

. . .

ANNE

No pets, either.

Pricilla opens her mouth to say something, but is interrupted by a loud thud on the patio door.

PRICILLA

(clasping her chest, startled)
Sweet gently swaddled Jesus!

Anne stands up and opens the blinds, revealing the patio. A large TRUMPETER SWAN is peering in the window, a bloated rat at its feet.

ANNE

Pricilla, meet Henry.

HENRY picks up the rat and throws it at the window again, leaving a splotch of slime and blood on the glass.

·   ·   ·

ANNE

Dick

STUART

Complete Dick

PRICILLA

(clucking her tongue)
I do declare! Such language.

Pricilla stands and walks to the window. As she bends over to get a closer look, Henry picks up the rat and throws it at the glass in front of Pricilla's face.

PRICILLA

My word! Well I never!

ANNE

We've tried everything. Trumpeters are protected, so we can't kill it. Fish and Wildlife won't touch it because the nesting grounds are so close.

. . .

Henry turns and poops down the glass.

PRICILLA
Hmmm. Charming.

Pricilla straightens up and draws the blinds.

PRICILLA
No matter. Minor hiccup.

We continue to hear bangs against the glass door.

STUART
It's hopeless.

Pricilla walks over and holds Anne and Stuart's hands.

PRICILLA
Oh, my lovelies. This bloody fowl has met his match.

. . .

CUT TO:

EXT. ANNE AND STUART'S HOUSE/FRONT WALKWAY-NIGHT

Anne and Stuart stand on the sidewalk in front of their home, dressed in formal attire. There is an OPEN HOUSE sign on the lawn.

STUART

I feel ridiculous wearing a suit to my own home.

ANNE

Pricilla said this was fancy. She is targeting the well-to-dos, and they expect a champagne and caviar affair.

CUT TO:

INT. ANNE AND STUART'S HOUSE/LIVING ROOM-NIGHT

. . .

Anne and Stuart walk through the living room. The house is full of people in formal wear. Everyone is laughing and chatting, champagne is being served on trays.

Anne and Stuart continue through the kitchen and out onto the patio overlooking the lake. There is a large table covered in food. In the center of the table is a silver platter with a large, garnished fowl.

GUEST (O.S.)
Isn't it just divine! The house is simply exquisite, and then this? This meat is to die for!

Pricilla walks up to Anne and Stuart, smirking.

ANNE
(whispering, anxious)
Is that Henry?!

STUART
(also whispering, and looking around at the crowd)

You can't kill a swan!

Pricilla grins and takes a sip of champagne.

PRICILLA

That's the thing, my dears. I didn't.

Pricilla points over the patio to the yard below. Sitting on the lawn, licking what appears to be a long, severed neck, is a white poodle wearing a pink collar decorated with rhinestones.

PRICILLA

Henry may have been a dick...
(whispers, giggling)
...but my Petunia is a cunt.

Pricilla walks away, laughing maniacally, and tosses a piece of meat in her mouth.

FADE OUT.

DESTINY RIDES A POLE

Ava wrinkled her nose at the smell as soon as she stepped inside the strip club. It smelled like stale cigarette smoke, cheap cologne, and deli meat. She didn't know why the club smelled like a Subway sandwich shop, but it did—chemical and meaty—and it was the reason she could never stomach a five-dollar footlong.

She searched the room and nodded when she found Destiny. Destiny was center stage, her preferred location, and she was the only stripper with anyone around. It was two o'clock in the afternoon, and while strip clubs in Reno didn't seem to do bad business at any time of the day, two o'clock was generally dead. The lunch buffet closed at one, and few of the tourists were awake and ready to party. The clientele at that hour consisted of a few crusty locals and a gang of geeked-out bachelor party stiffs who had been too cheap to spring for the classy trip to Vegas.

Destiny was on her hands and knees, grinding the stage to a Whitesnake song. She threw back her head and let the wild mane of red hair whip back suggestively. She grinned when she saw Ava, winked, then turned her attention back to the drunk in the front and his wad of dollar bills. When the song was over, Destiny got a lively round of applause and some whistles from her admirers. She left the money on the slick black stage, apparently unconcerned, then exited stage left. Ava followed.

When they got backstage, Destiny hugged Ava and kissed her soundly. She didn't bother getting dressed. She sat down in her chair in front of her make-up station, nude from the waist up. Ava paid no attention.

"Thanks for coming so quickly. It's been a while. You look good," Destiny said. She looked Ava up and down and grinned.

"Thanks. No problem. You have a job?" Ava asked.

"Professional. To the point. I like that. I've always admired your work ethic," Destiny said.

"Maybe she just doesn't want to stare at your titties." Another stripper, in her mid-thirties with brown hair and wearing a blue Victoria's Secret satin bra and panty set paired with black spike heels walked in. A C-section scar ran along her lower abdomen and she had ample stretch marks. She threw a silk kimono at Destiny and scowled.

"Everybody wants to stare at my titties," Destiny laughed. "Stop being so grumpy."

The woman rolled her eyes. "You think awfully much of them, that's for sure." The woman regarded Ava. "Ava. How are you?"

"Fine, Sharon. How's things with you?" Ava nodded politely.

"Same as always," Sharon said.

"Ava. Last job, huh?" A short blonde entered the room. She was dressed in a Catholic school girl uniform. She hugged Ava then sat next to Sharon.

"Hello, Jane. Should be the last one, yep," Ava nodded.

"We'll see," a gravelly voice said. The old woman puffed out a long plume of cigarette smoke and heaved her considerable bulk into a chair. Her thick, black polyester pants strained against her as she settled into the chair and crossed her legs. She yanked down her sensible floral print blouse so it covered her stomach and looked over her bifocals at Ava. "Job isn't done yet. And you still owe."

"Betty." Ava nodded politely and hoped that her desire to set Betty on fire did not show on her face. For two thousand years, Betty had been a hateful bitch.

She was rude and never missed an opportunity to remind anyone of how much they owed on their contract. "You're looking… fit." Ava said.

"Can it. I look fucking fat and old. Happens to everyone." Betty stubbed out her smoke and lit another, then grabbed a walkie talkie from her belt and screamed into it. "Goddamn it, Dale, I said none of that rap shit. Tell Charity to get another act. Turn that shit off." She didn't wait for a response before turning her attention back to Ava. "We'll see if you got the stomach for this one."

"I've never shirked a task," Ava said as she bristled. It wasn't wise to throw attitude at any of the women in the room, but Ava had enough crap from them over the years. She had never once failed to deliver, but Betty always said there was a first time for everything. Ava knew that to be true. Two thousand years of watching humans had taught her that almost anything was possible where they were concerned. But Ava wasn't human—at least not anymore—and she had never given them cause to doubt her integrity. She signed her contract and she did her job, every time. The hateful old bitty couldn't deny it.

"Of course, you haven't," Destiny cooed. She got up from the chair and put her arm around Ava. "This is all silly."

"Yeah, let's celebrate," Jane said. She stood on

Ava's other side. "It's been a long time since I've seen anyone on their last job."

"You've never seen anyone on their last job," Sharon said.

"Well, you're seeing it today," Ava said. She stared at Sharon and at Betty, both of whom looked doubtful. "What's the job?"

Destiny nodded at Jane, who nodded back. She rummaged around in a wardrobe and pulled out a black briefcase. She held it out to Ava. "Should I open it? Do you want to see who it is before you accept?"

That was protocol. Ava had the right to look it over and decide if she really wanted to take the job. She had never once refused a job, not even the vilest ones. She had poisoned whole families. Taken little children, teens on the cusp of adulthood, mothers and fathers, and respected elders. Nobody ever escaped her, and she had never once questioned why they were in the case. Not everyone was able to do that. She knew colleagues that refused to kill children or good people, and they paid the price. They had been tortured and given another thousand years' service. It wasn't a bond broken lightly, and it certainly wasn't a bond broken on your last job, no matter who was in the case.

Ava shook her head. She grasped the handle, and when she did, the case glowed and pulsed. She felt the familiar stinging in her hand as the handle grew hotter.

She held tight as it burned into her flesh, searing her skin and smoking. The pain only lasted a few seconds before it abated, and was replaced by a cool, refreshing feeling, as if somebody had spread aloe on the burn.

"Thanks. I'll take care of it," Ava said. She left the club, and when she got home, she opened the case. Marisol Diaz smirked at her from the newspaper clippings and press releases. She was a former Reno city council member who had progressed to the Nevada state legislature and was now running for US Senator. She was in a tough fight with the old, incumbent white guy. A single mother and former Reno cocktail waitress, Marisol made a name for herself with real talk and progressive ideas that frightened the people in love with the status quo. But times were changing, and as the demographics changed with them, she gained support and momentum. It terrified the Establishment.

Ava frowned. She had listened to a few speeches, and the news channels followed the race religiously. Marisol had style, charisma, and good ideas. If Ava took her out, it might stifle progress and set the state of Nevada back twenty years. But a deal was a deal.

She began her process. She researched, looked at every Facebook post, every Tweet, every Instagram. She poured through personal records, credit reports, bank statements. Almost every time, she could find something to hate about the person and that made it easier. This time, she found a funny, smart, tough woman who made mistakes and didn't always make good choices, but it was clear from the research and facts that Marisol had always made progress. To Ava, Marisol's potential seemed limitless. The media and Democratic National Committee felt the same, because they were fighting hard to elect her. Ava watched every single second of coverage as she prepared to do the job and found it painful to do so. For the first time, she was conflicted, and she couldn't have picked a worse time for it. She stalled and hedged, and after a month of inaction, she received a summons from the ladies.

"What's the hold up?" Betty croaked around her cigarette?

"I'm doing research. It's a tough job," Ava shrugged.

"Oh, sugar, we know it's not an easy task," Destiny said as she hugged Ava. "That's why it's yours."

"If it was easy, we would have given it to a newbie," Sharon said. She scrubbed a stain off one of Jane's pleated plaid mini-skirts. "Jesus, Jane, soak it sooner next time."

"I know you can do it," Jane said. "You're the best, and this is your last job."

"Yeah, about that. You're sure this is what you want? You didn't make a mistake?" Ava tried to sound casual, but never in a thousand years had she ever asked that question.

"We don't make mistakes. Her number came up. So do your job. It isn't negotiable." Betty said. She looked over her glasses at Ava. "You know what happens if you don't."

"I know," Ava snapped back.

"Of course, sugar, you always have a choice," Destiny cooed. "It's just the consequences that get you."

"No, there is no choice. We all know that," Sharon said.

"I just asked if there was an alternative. If there's not, there's not," Ava said. "I'll get something done. Bye."

"Now, now, no need to be testy," Jane said.

"Sugar, you do what you have to do. It will work itself out," Destiny said as she walked Ava out.

Ava waited patiently in the kitchen. She called out the order for table 48, the one with Marisol Diaz and the top Democratic strategists. She made certain that all the food was perfectly placed on the plate. She also made certain that the gastrique had enough poison to kill a hundred people. Marisol Diaz would be dead in under a minute. It would be fast, but unfortunately not painless. Ava took no joy in the task as she loaded up the plates and carried them to the table.

"We're still five points behind in the polls. Now, you know there's a margin of error, but it's not looking good, Marisol," the woman said. Ava guessed she oversaw the campaign. She put a plate down in front of the woman.

"I don't believe it," Marisol said. "We're close, and I know we're going to win. People want the change. Patterson is a racist. He admitted it."

"You're right, but, it's more complicated than that. We have to prepare ourselves for alternatives to winning."

"Nice way of saying losing," Marisol said. "I won't accept that. I won't accept Patterson as a representative for us."

"He is a piece of shit, for sure, but we talked about this Marisol. Sometimes that doesn't matter."

"I don't accept that. It does matter. We have to make it matter." Marisol's eyes flashed and she slammed her fist down on the table.

Ava knew everything about her, the good, the bad, everything. She'd seen a lot of people in this position and none of them were quite like Marisol. She could make a difference. Was that why they wanted her dead? It was complex. She knew that, but right there, in that moment, the choice was simple. It was her last job.

Ava looked at Marisol and smiled. Marisol smiled

back up at her. She set the plate of food down on the table in front of Marisol.

"Can I get you anything else?" she asked.

Marisol smiled and shook her head. "No thanks."

"Hey, good luck in your election. I know you're going to change things," Ava said.

"I hope so, yeah. We can. We all can," Marisol said. "Thanks for your support."

Ava nodded and walked back in the kitchen and out the back. She took an Uber back to the strip club.

"Done," she said as she handed the briefcase back to Betty.

"You had a choice though," Destiny said as she smiled sadly.

"I did. I'm good with it," Ava said.

"The pain will be terrible," Jane said.

"Are you sure you can take it?" Sharon asked.

"Do I have a choice?" Ava asked. She threw her head back and screamed as manacles of blue flame erupted from the floor and latched around her wrists and ankles. The floor shimmered and liquified into foul-smelling tar. The chains pulled tight and retracted, pulling Ava slowly through the tar. Her skin bubbled and seared as she sank below the surface.

"Always," the four women said in unison.

PRECISELY

"How was school today?" I asked her as she ate the peanut butter and jelly sandwich. The crusts were removed, and the sandwich cut into two perfect right triangles, just how she liked. She wouldn't touch that sandwich had the cuts not been precise. Once I hadn't squared off the bread before I made the diagonal and she cried for four hours.

"Fine," Gracie said around a mouthful of sandwich. She placed the sandwich down carefully on the plate. I didn't measure it, but I knew that if I had measured, it would be equidistant from the sides of the square plate. Gracie picked up the frosty glass of milk and washed down her bite of peanut butter.

"Just fine? You had a spelling test today, right? We

studied last night." I sat down on the bar stool across the wide kitchen island.

"Yes. We had the test. I got a hundred." The grade wouldn't be posted until Friday but there was no doubt in Gracie's voice. "We had a spelling bee too. I won."

"Of course you did," I said. "You knew those words backwards and forwards."

"Yes. I did," she said. She set the glass of milk down precisely in the center of the coaster, directly on the wet ring of condensation it had already left.

"You have homework tonight?" I asked.

"Yes. I have twelve subtraction problems to finish and I have 27 pages to read for language arts," she said.

"Oh, well that's not much," I said. "Why don't you go outside and play for an hour or so?"

Gracie shook her head. "No. There's an 87% chance of rain and the wind is from the northwest at 14 miles per hour. I'd prefer to play inside today."

"Okay, sure," I nodded. I knew that she would be right about the chance of rain. She always knew. I didn't need to consult the weather report to verify.

"May I color?" she asked.

"Certainly," I said.

Gracie finished her sandwich and milk. She rinsed the plate and glass exactly three times. She knew that if she did it three times, it would cover 99% of the surface area. I didn't know how she knew that, Google or YouTube or something, but she knew. She placed the plate and glass in the dishwasher, then closed it. We walked up the stairs to her playroom. All the toys were lined up precisely on shelves or sorted into baskets by type and color. Her Barbie dolls were housed in clear plastic cases.

Gracie went to the bookshelf and selected a coloring book.

"I think I'll color fairytale princesses today," Gracie said. She pulled her crayons out of the art cabinet and opened the box. They were all sharpened, evenly worn, and arranged by color.

"Cool." I sat down on the white loveseat.

"Oh, I forgot my smock," Gracie said. She got up and went to the closet.

"It's probably ok. You're just using crayons," I said.

She looked at me for a moment and her face looked horrified. She shook her head as she donned her art smock and buttoned it. "No. I always wear my smock."

"Yeah, but I'm just saying you don't have to wear it. Not for crayons."

"No." Her face grew dark and angry. She slapped the little wooden table three times. "I do have to wear it. You know I do have to wear it." She began to cry, and she kept hitting the table, each slap louder, harder, and faster than the last.

I jumped up and ran over to the table, then knelt down and smiled at her. "Hey… Gracie… okay, okay. It's fine. You're wearing your smock. Look, you've got it on." I pointed to her smock. "It's the one with kittens on it. Your Tuesday smock."

She looked down at it and saw the kittens and smiled. She stopped pounding the table and sucked in a big breath. "Yes. It's Tuesday. I'm wearing my Tuesday smock. I won't have a problem."

I nodded. "Right. Tuesday smock. No problem." I smiled at her and pointed to the coloring book. "Who are you going to color today? Cinderella?"

She sat down at the table and sniffed a few times. Her tears were gone and her face went back to the unreadable mask it normally was. "No. Sleeping Beauty is next in the book." She opened the book and flipped to the next uncolored page. Sure enough, Sleeping Beauty reclined in her bed amidst roses and overgrown thorny vines. A spinning wheel with a single drop of blood coming from the spindle sat near the bed.

"Ah, yes, Briar Rose. I like that one." I pointed to the roses. "Roses are my favorite but I wouldn't want to sleep on thorns," I said.

"This one has blood." Gracie pointed to the drop

of blood. She selected the crayon she wanted—crimson red—and colored the blood first. "Blood doesn't stay red like that. Not when it dries."

"No, but it's just a picture." I sat down on the little chair next to hers.

"When blood dries it turns brown," she said. "Red-brown. If it's night, it looks black."

"Yes. Yes it does," I said. "What color will you make the roses?"

"I'll make them yellow. Like yours were," she said.

"Okay, that's good." A lump formed in my throat and I felt far away and flimsy, like I was a piece of sheer cloth blowing in the wind.

She colored carefully. There wasn't a stroke outside the lines. When she finished, she sharpened all her crayons and put them back. Gracie closed the coloring book and placed it in its spot on the bookshelf. She took off her Tuesday smock—it was immaculately clean—and put it in the dirty clothes hamper.

"Daddy will be home in thirty-six minutes," she said. She never looked at the clock. I didn't either. I knew that she was correct. He was always on time. "I'm going to do my homework, then I'll check everything."

"Okay," I said. I didn't argue that she didn't need to check anything. She would do it anyway. She did all her math homework and finished her reading in twelve minutes. The math problems were all correct and they were perfectly drawn in pencil. No mistakes. No hesitations. She read the twenty-seven pages of Grimm's Fairytales. I thought it was an odd choice for school reading. It was the original, not the watered-down Disney versions of the tales. Violent and bloody.

"I chose it," she said. "Mrs. Combs let us pick our own this week."

"They're very scary," I said. "Are you okay?"

She looked at me and nodded. "Of course. They're only make-believe."

She put her folders and book in her backpack. She carried it downstairs and placed it on the table next to the hall tree. Everything had a place. The backpack always sat on the left side of the occasional table, ready for her to take the next morning. She checked it twice and adjusted it so that it was lined up with the side of the table. She straightened her coat that hung on the peg in the mudroom.

"Daddy will be home in seven minutes," she said. I could hear a slight panic in her voice. She was worried she didn't have enough time to check everything before he came home.

"You have time, Gracie. You have plenty of time."

"I know that I have time," she said in a huffy voice.

She straightened her dress and marched into the kitchen. She checked every cabinet and made sure that everything inside was neatly stored. She walked into the pantry and adjusted all of the canned goods so that the labels lined up and faced outward.

In the bathroom, she checked the hand towels and made sure they hung equidistant from the towel rack. She opened the toilet lid and flushed it three times. She made a pass through the hallway and checked that nothing was out of place. Gracie stood next to the hall tree and waited. Sweat beaded up on her forehead and she straightened her dress nervously.

"One minute," she whispered. "Don't fidget," she said. She wasn't speaking to me. She was reminding herself.

He walked in the door exactly one minute later. He hung up his laptop bag on its designated peg and his overcoat as well. He looked over everything in the hallway and nodded. When he finally regarded Gracie, he frowned. "You were crying."

"I haven't been crying," Gracie said in a small, flat voice.

"You're lying. You were crying. I see stains on your collar. Your dress is askew. Straighten it."

He never asked her why she had been crying and her dress wasn't messed up at all. I felt the rage start to boil in me, low and deep. I felt hot and far away this time, overly large, not flimsy, and I balled up my fists. I did my best to control it, but the world started to vibrate and seemed to speed up.

I looked over at Gracie and she was watching me, her face white and terrified. That calmed me and I stopped and exhaled slowly as I willed the rage ball to recede back into its cave.

"Everything's good Gracie. Don't worry," I said.

"Is your mother home yet?" He asked as he looked through the mail.

Gracie was still looking at me and I winked at her.

"Karen will be home in twelve minutes," Gracie said.

"Don't call her Karen!" he screamed. "Go to your room. Your mother will call you for dinner," he thundered.

Gracie nodded. "Dinner will be ready in thirty-two minutes." She started up the steps to the second story.

"Yes. Yes it will," he said, then he went back to sorting the mail. The hatred I had for him seethed in me but I left him alone and followed Gracie up to her room. She sat on her bed and read a book. Another copy of fairy tales.

"Which one are you reading now?" I asked as I sat down beside her.

"Jack and the Beanstalk. The giant dies. He falls and breaks his neck." She pointed to a grotesque illustration. The giant's head was twisted and his neck lumpy where it broke in the fall.

"That's a really gross picture," I said. "Don't you want to read a nice story for a change?"

"There are no nice stories," Gracie said. She flipped through the pages until she got to the Little Red Riding Hood story. "I like this one. There's blood when the woodsman cuts open the wolf. It's not as much blood as you had though. It's not an accurate representation," she said.

"That's not a nice thing for you to think about," I said. "Why don't you try thinking about something else?"

"Karen is home," she said.

"It's better if you call her Mom," I said. "Your dad will be less mad."

"He'll always be mad. Like he was at you," Gracie said. "Her name is Karen. It's fair." She looked agitated. Her face was angry and red and she began to open and shut the book repeatedly in an increasingly hysterical rhythm.

"You're right. That's her name. Everything is okay," I whispered.

She stopped banging the book around and looked at me. "It doesn't feel okay," she whispered back.

"I know, but it is. I won't let it not be okay. Not ever."

Gracie stared at me a moment and I watched her calm down. She went back to reading her book. When they called for her, she went downstairs and ate her dinner without any complaints. She came back upstairs after and got ready for bed. She smoothed the crisp white duvet cover back so it was perfectly aligned on the bed. She lay exactly in the middle. I didn't need to measure.

She yawned and looked over at me. "You'll stay? All night?"

I nodded. "You know that I will."

"I know," she said. "Goodnight Mom."

She turned off the little bedside lamp and closed her eyes. Her hands were folded precisely over her stomach. When her breathing evened out, her little face relaxed and for the first time in twenty-four hours, she looked like a normal six-year-old. Peaceful.

That always made me want to cry. I felt weird and wispy and far away again, but I stayed right there by the bed.

She'd be awake in exactly eight hours. Neither of us needed the alarm.

TRUE NORTH

"Republican or Democrat?"

June swallowed her food, and choked out, "Canadian."

Until that point, it had been a normal day: errands, writing, then lunch with a few friends —Charmaine, Amber, and Amber's son Lester. They had decided on Pho, settling on a quaint but lovely spot. After some awesome conversation and a few bites of delicious food, the woman approached. Who was she? None of them knew. This stranger dropped her purse in the middle of the table and spewed out the loaded question.

After June's response and curt answers from Amber, she left as abruptly as she came—alone, without speaking to anyone else, or even leaving with food.

"What do you suppose that was about?" Amber asked.

"Odd, that," Charmaine said. "She didn't speak to anyone else."

A chill ruffled the fine hair on June's arms. *Odd, indeed,* she thought, pushing her food around the plate with her chopsticks.

No thought was given to the stranger for the rest of the meal. Laughs were had, plans were made, and the bill paid.

"Italian next time?" Amber said.

June and Charmaine agreed, and the three bid each other adieu. It had mostly been a wonderful lunch.

Mostly.

Something irksome lingered in the folds of June's brain as she took long strides to her car, the glare of a thousand eyes boring into her flesh. She crossed the parking lot and jumped into her vehicle with great gusto, slamming the door hard enough to rattle both the windows and her nerves.

What is wrong with me?

Laughing it off, June stabbed the key in the ignition and fired up the car, craving music to drown out the worry in her mind. As she looked ahead to pull out of her parking spot, she locked eyes with a woman walking her dog—*a Labrador Retriever, I think.*

The woman stared at June. So did the dog. As they passed the vehicle, both heads turned, craning around even as they cleared the back bumper, both woman and dog refusing to break eye-contact. The woman mouthed words that June made out with crystal clarity:

Republican or Democrat?

By the time they had rounded the corner out of view, June was trembling.

Get it together.

Drawing a calming breath deep into her belly, June pulled out of the spot and proceeded toward the grocery store, her last intended stop before heading home. Though only a few miles away, the drive took longer than usual, for no good reason. Traffic was sparse, the weather overcast but sensible, and the route was clear. But the journey lingered, taking hours and hours, time Jane spent in her own head, hearing thousands of voices, feeling thousands of eyes staring…

Kroger was virtually empty; nobody preferred to shop on a Tuesday afternoon. June felt better once she was under the twitching fluorescent lighting and speakers softly cooing 90s pop hits. Perusing the aisles felt normal, peaceful, with no eyes or voices invading her space. As she perused the selection of cereal for her son, a chill washed over her once again.

She was not alone in the aisle. She could feel it, hear it. Looking to one end, she saw no one. Looking to the other, she found the same. No one there but her and the cereal, those cartoon characters and manic colors peddling their sugary wares. The box in her hand grew warm, squirming to life between her fingers.

"Republican or Democrat?"

Her stomach flipped as Count Chocula spoke, his voice like nails down a chalkboard. His eyes searched her face, his sharp-toothed smile widening into a ferocious grin.

"Canadian," June squeaked beneath her breath.

June dropped the cereal. With her tension at the snapping point, the noise of the box hitting the floor might as well have been cymbals inside her skull. June abandoned her cart and hurried to the exit. The music above her had stopped, and silence swallowed the store. She passed by the registers, which now had long lineups snaking down the aisles. Row upon row of people, lips clenched in tight lines, all eyes on June. Her step slowed and softened until she was tiptoeing to her destination without knowing why. They could see her —their eyes followed her, their heads turning ever so slightly with each step she took.

Mesmerized by the mob, June didn't see the large man blocking the automatic doors. She bumped into him, knocking a short burst of a scream from her belly.

"Oh, I'm terribly sorry. I just…"

He was tall, almost filling the doorway, with a black bowler hat perched on his bulbous head. He wore a flowing trench coat and carried a heavy cane topped with an intricate carving of a goat. His eyes were dark and shadowed, resting deep in his skull. His air tasted of meat and ash and sulphur.

"Republican or democrat?" His voice was a moist growl.

"Canadian." June was crying now, her heart a heavy rock in her throat.

Though he was tall as a tree, he was frail, no more than a sculpture of bones holding up that trench coat. She pushed him over and ran past him through the door. Day had become night, the winds howling, bringing with them a sheath of black clouds. She reached her car, fumbling for her keys, and was just about safely behind her steering wheel when she noticed the bright orange flyer under her windshield wiper. She snatched it and smeared the tears out of her eyes so she could read the delicately scribed message:

Republican or Democrat?

Tires squealing, June fishtailed out of the parking

lot as the obese clouds gave way, dropping rain in great sheets over her windshield. . The world around the car was obsidian, the rain like falling meteors in the beams of her headlights. She drove for hours, wishing her house to appear, her fireplace, a good book, and a glass of bourbon waiting for her. But instead, a light in the distance flickered, a neon beacon in the storm.

It was the Pho restaurant, its neon sign flashing.

How did I get back here?

She was parked right back where she had been before. But there was no one else—no other cars, no one seated at the tables inside. The rain had stopped, the wind had stilled, and the world outside had turned a muted grey. All of it. The green trees, her red car. Everything a grey nothingness.

As if floating on a cloud, she stepped out of her car and went to the door of the restaurant. She pulled it open, and the good-luck cat chime hanging from the jamb announced her arrival. In its tinny, tinkling chime, it spoke to her:

Republicanordemocrat?Republicanordemocrat? Republicanordemocrat?

Canadian.

She had been mistaken. There *were* people in the restaurant. She hadn't seen them from the window, but she hadn't had a clear view of the table they were seated at. Her table. The table she and Charmaine and Amber had eaten and laughed and chatted at just moments before. June approached the table and took a seat opposite a small man with dark eyes and a long, braided white beard. Beside him was her, face down on the table, bloated and blue.

"Ah, my dear June," he said, his words followed by a wheezing laugh full of nicotine and whiskey.

June couldn't speak. All she could do was stare at the body on the table—blue flesh, eyes solid red, and hands clasped at her throat.

"Spring roll," the man said, sipping his tea. "Choked on my spring roll. Too small, I make them."

Water from the ornamental fountain trickled, cathartic in the silent, impossibly still restaurant. Outside the windows, the fires of hell burned with vigor and the white feathers of heaven swirled down from above.

"So," he said, taking a bite of the deadly spring roll. "Republican or Democrat?"

"Uh..."

Nothing. Her heart no longer beat against her chest, her throat was no longer clenched, and her face had dried of tears and sorrow.

"Canadian."

She spoke her decision with authority. A firm certainty. He stared at her a moment, his fingers teasing the tip of his beard before nodding his resignation.

"Very well."

A door appeared in the wall, a door that hadn't been there before. A feather upset by a draft, she floated towards the door, pressing through to the other side.

It was a sight to behold—one that revived her heart and invigorated her soul: screaming mountains, emerald lakes, sparkling snow and rosy cheeks. Moose nibbled on Timbits in the distance and Mounties fried bannock over an open fire.

June smiled and walked home.

WAITING FOR TAMMY ALBRECHT

The sign on the table said, "RESERVED FOR TAMMY ALBRECHT". Jack didn't know who Tammy Albrecht was, but it was a great table, overlooking the man-made pond they used to train scuba divers. Somebody found a mammoth skull there twenty years ago, and since then they sunk all kinds of junk for the divers to practice with: cars, a Sherman Tank, the monument head of Stephen F. Austin. He could see them finishing up dives for the day. The early evening sun was dipping below the tree line and reflecting blue and gold off the water. It was a nice place to sit and have a drink, which was probably why Tammy Albrecht had reserved it.

A woman sat down at the table too. She was

drinking an Old Fashioned. Jack was always wary of women who liked bourbon. They were unpredictable.

The woman looked at the sign and read it as she sipped her drink. She looked over and examined Jack carefully before she spoke.

"Are you waiting for Tammy Albrecht?" the woman asked.

"No." Jack replied. "Are you Tammy Albrecht?"

"No," she said. "What kind of person sits at a reserved table?"

"Maybe you should ask yourself the same question," Jack said, more defensively than he intended. "You're not Tammy Albrecht."

"Just because I said I wasn't Tammy Albrecht doesn't mean I'm not waiting for her." She sipped her drink and watched him carefully.

"Are you waiting for Tammy Albrecht?" Jack asked.

She smiled. "No," she said.

His face reddened. He shook his head and went back to his drink.

"I'm going to laugh like I think you're funny," she said.

"What if I *am* funny?" Jack asked as he sipped his whiskey.

"Tell me a joke then," she said.

"What? Now?"

"You said you were funny," she said.

"No, I said what if I really am funny?"

"I don't think we're in danger of being confused about that," she said. "You can't tell a joke."

"Who tells a joke on demand?" Jack asked.

"Comedians," she said dryly.

"Well, then you should have hijacked a table reserved at The Laugh Factory."

The woman did laugh then, a loud, genuine belly laugh that made both smile.

"See, I told you I was funny," Jack said. "I think maybe you're unhinged."

She nodded. "It's likely." She sipped her drink. They watched the divers in the pond and drank in silence for a few moments. "Why would you want to dive in that pond?"

"I heard they found a mammoth head in there once," Jack shrugged.

"And they're looking for another one?" She rolled her eyes. "They dumped some old cars and busted up concrete in there. Who wants to see that?"

"They're learning to dive," Jack explained.

"I'd rather learn to dive someplace the neighborhood sewage didn't drain in to," she said. She finished her drink and signaled for the waiter to bring her another.

"You don't know that," Jack said.

"What? That I don't want to learn to scuba dive in raw sewage? I do know that."

"You know what I meant. You don't know there's sewage in there. Also, it's weird."

"It's not," she shook her head. "This is too far outside the city limits to have city sewers. They all have leach beds. Runs right down the hill and into Turd Lake there." She motioned to the water.

"No, it's weird that you brought up that particular topic of conversation with a total stranger," Jack said. He finished his own drink and signaled for another.

"It's not weird. It's just factual." She sighed. "I had to do it to try and figure you out."

"What does that even mean?" Jack asked. He eyed her Old Fashioned. Strange Women and Bourbon. His theory was true yet again.

"It's just a way to get to know you," she said.

"Or… you could, I don't know, ask a person questions about themselves," Jack countered.

"That's how most people do it. I'm not most people," she said.

"Clearly."

"So, here's what I know. You are the kind of person who sits at a table reserved for somebody else. Also, you're uncomfortable with factual discussions about sewage treatment."

"Oh wow," he said. "Your powers of deduction rival Sherlock Holmes."

"You're drinking whiskey neat, which is not entirely the correct way to do it, but that means you're not a hipster, which, I already knew from your pants; They're not rolled up or too tight on your crotch." She nodded and cocked her head as she looked him over again. "And you haven't gotten up and left yet." She sipped her drink and grinned, a satisfied look on her face.

He said nothing, just stared at her. He hadn't gotten up and left yet. That was true. She was weird, but she wasn't boring, and her eyes weren't the blue he thought they were. They were an interesting shade of violet that he had never seen before. They danced with amusement.

"Is this your typical Friday evening? You come out here, wait for Tammy Albrecht, and bother strangers?" He tried to sound annoyed, but his smile betrayed him.

"I told you, I'm not waiting for Tammy Albrecht."

"Well I'm not waiting for her either," he said.

"Then why are we still here?" She said as she took a long, slow drink of her bourbon.

CLOSE ENOUGH

lank.

The sound of metal on metal jarred Zoe out of a heavy sleep. A shooting pain radiated from the back of her neck to the edge of her temple. She rolled on her back, peeling her cheek off sticky wood.

Where am I?

A floor?

She sat up, no small feat through the bellow of complaints of at least a dozen screaming, aching muscles. She felt like she had been through the wringer and back. Still lingering in the throes of a deep slumber, she was discombobulated and fuzzy. She rubbed her eyes, attempting to free her vision of haze and the grit of sleep.

It was dark as black; Zoe couldn't make out her hand in front of her face.

Your other senses, Zoe. You have four. Use them.

Breathing deep, she was overwhelmed by the scent of wood, metal, and all manner of bodily fluids.

Her heart rate sped from a trot to a sprint. Time for a thorough self-examination. She was wearing a t-shirt and panties but nothing else. Aches whispered to her—ghosts of a recent struggle. She searched her wrists and ankles, expecting ropes, cuffs, restraints…

Why do I expect to find those?

I've been taken.

There was nothing binding her, but her hands slid over her bare legs, wet and slick.

She tasted her fingers. They were salty, metallic…

Blood.

Panic sunk its nails into her chest, constricting her lungs and clenching her heart.

She had to get out.

Frantic, Zoe scoured the walls, groping the wood panels and protruding two-by-fours, searching for a door, a light switch, anything that might aid in illumination or escape. Finding nothing on the perimeter, she extended her arms in front of her and shuffled to the middle of the room.

"Hello?" Her voice barely rose above the volume of her breathing.

Grunts and clanks answered, bouncing around the room, rattling in her skull. Zoe hesitated, unsure of which way to go, when a chain brushed her hair.

Light.

She pulled it, and amber light flooded the room, struggling to glow through a dirty naked bulb in the ceiling.

The room was a large coffin, barren wood-framed walls. *An attic,* Zoe thought, *and it's empty.*

Just about.

There was a wooden closet on the wall with a slide lock barring the door from the outside. There was a what looked to be a mail slot cut into the door, with dark brown stains spilling from it and trailing down the wood like tears.

With the introduction of light came an explosion of sound: keening and wailing from behind the door and the clashing of metal and wood in violent conflict. Zoe backed away and spotted a gleam of metal in her peripheral. A silver handle on the floor glimmered under the light like beacon of freedom. She took a step toward the attic door, but the agony of the other prisoner halted her escape.

Slender fingers crawled through the slot, hooking over the edge. The fingers were clearly broken, contorted this way and that, and the nails caked with blood.

Got a good piece of him, she did.

"It's okay," Zoe whispered. "I'll be back. I'll get help."

The hands pushed through the opening, the appendages themselves begging for help.

That's when Zoe saw the bracelet.

"Michaela?"

A braided rainbow friendship bracelet, fastened with duct tape, dangled from the slender wrist poking through the door.

Refastened with duct tape.

Zoe looked down at her own copy of the friendship bracelet, brown, saturated in blood.

"Help," Zoe said, her head bobbing in agreement with her own plan. "I'll get help."

A million thoughts assaulted her as she lunged for the attic door.

What if the kidnapper is still here?

What if he kills me? Kills us?

She didn't care. She dropped the ladder, intent on breaking out of her prison and bringing help back for her best friend. But she stopped one step down the ladder.

Michaela. She had loved Michaela all her life. Friends since childhood, they had done everything together. College, marriage, careers, babies. Zoe had never been without Michaela. She simply could not live without her.

Wouldn't live without her.

She couldn't leave her behind. Not even for a moment, not to get help. *Whoever did this might come back and kill her.*

Zoe ran to Michaela's door and slid open the latch. As the door creaked open, Michaela's cries subsided.

Michaela was shackled to the wall in iron cuffs that reached just as far as the door. She was swollen and broken, her body all shades of purple and yellow with bruises old and new alike. She had gag shoved in her mouth.

She's not quite right ... but close enough.

"C'mon Michaela, let's get out—"

But something was wrong. Michaela shook her head. She backed up against the wall and crouched on her haunches, cowering in the corner like a beaten puppy.

"No more, please," she said. Whimpers turned to screams. She pushed herself as far into the cell as she could. "You psychotic bitch! I'm not Michaela! She's never coming back!"

Like a sledgehammer had struck her chest, Zoe backed away. She couldn't catch her breath. She couldn't cry, couldn't scream, couldn't think. As if floating in a haze, she moved to the attic stairs and descended to the house below.

Her house.

Face to face with the mirror in the hall, she looked at the reflection; she stared at the blood on her clothes, the claw marks on her arms. She flexed her knuckles, which were battered and bruised. A clump of hair from her best friend's replacement was hanging down, tangled in the friendship bracelet on her arm.

And a monster stared back at her, smiling.

SURE WAS

The door to the Empress Saloon flung open and a wide load by the name of Bunk Billings burst through the entrance.

"I'm looking for Quick Billy Banks and by God, I'm gonna kill that son of a bitch!" Bunk Billings yelled as he hitched up his gun belt, slicked down his thick walrus mustache, and stuck out his fat gunt.

Billy Banks leaned against the bar and finished his beer. He set the glass down, turned to face the man, and tipped his hat back on his head as he studied him.

The man was fat. Billy didn't reckon he knew of a horse in town that could hold the man, he was so big. Maybe a draft horse from one of the dirt scratchers could do it, but that horse would have a sway when he was through, to be sure.

Every head in the bar stared at them. They all knew who Billy was, and now the fat man did too. Billy didn't know the fat man. He would have remembered a fellow that round had he ever run afoul of him before.

"You Quick Billy Banks?" Bunk Billings pointed at Billy. Everyone scooted away. The bartender scurried from behind the bar and the piano player packed up his kit and hid in a corner. The whores all shut their doors whether they were busy or not.

"Who wants to know?" Billy said. He leaned casually back against the bar and smiled. His tone was friendly.

"I want to know," Bunk Billings said. His face was beet red and big rivulets of sweat ran down his cheeks and into the mutton chops which accentuated his piggy jowls.

"You said that already, friend. I asked you your name," Billy replied.

"I ain't your friend, you son of a bitch! My name is Bunk Billings, and I'm the man that's gonna by God kill you."

The fat man went for his gun but before his gun ever cleared the holster, Billy pulled his Colt and shot the big bastard right between the eyes. He fell over with a solid thump and the whole saloon shook. Once the dust settled, everyone went back to what they were doing before. Billy walked over to the man and gave him a good look. He didn't know him at all. He shrugged. People were crazy.

"Why'd you have to kill him in here, Billy?" The bartender kicked at the dead man and motioned towards the door. "How am I supposed to drag a big 'un like that out of here?"

"I didn't have no choice, Bob. That big bastard drew on me. What was I supposed to do? Let him plug me?"

"Well what did he want to kill you for?" Bob the bartender crossed his arms as they looked down at the corpse.

"Hell if I know," Billy said. "I never seen him before."

"You musta done something to him to rile him like that."

"Well I didn't," Billy said. He was starting to get annoyed, and the fat man smelled like shit. "I'd remember a lard like that."

"How am I gonna get him out of here? He's already stinking."

"Pay them whores to do it. I'd wager they know a thing or two about dragging a fatty like that outside." Billy pointed to the table of ladies who eyed him.

"I don't even know if he'll fit through the door." Bob looked worried.

"For Christ's sake, Bob, he came in the door didn't he?" Billy reached into his vest pocket and pulled out two gold pieces. He flung one at the whores and one at Bob. "I don't wanna hear no more about it." He left it at that. Billy stepped over the fat man as he left the Empress. He mounted his horse and rode off back to the cow camp for the evening.

The door to the Empress Saloon flung open and a wide load by the name of Bunk Billings burst through the entrance.

"I'm looking for Quick Billy Banks and by God, I'm gonna kill that son of a bitch!" Bunk Billings hitched up his gun belt, slicked down his walrus mustache, and stuck out his fat gunt.

Billy Banks leaned against the bar and finished his beer. He set the glass down, turned to face the man, and tipped his hat back on his head as he studied him.

He'd seen this fat cuss before but he couldn't recall just exactly where. Eagle Pass maybe. Doyle's Gap. He was familiar, but then again if you'd ever seen a man so fat he had to have been the reason they invented double doors, you'd remember him.

"Who wants to know?" Billy asked, his tone friendly as he smiled.

"I'm Bunk Billings and by God, I'm gonna kill you, you son of a bitch!"

Bunk Billings got his gun out, but before his fat fingers could squeeze the trigger, Billy had pulled his Colt, shot the fat man dead, and holstered before the massive man hit the floor.

"He's too fat. I'll never get him out the door," Bob the bartender yelled. He kicked the corpse and watched it jiggle.

"He came in the door, didn't he?" Billy said. He felt strange, like he'd said those exact words before.

"Well, yes, but he's big. I ain't dragging him."

Billy reached into his pocket and pulled out two gold pieces. He flung one at Bob and one at the gaggle of whores who gathered to watch the spectacle. "Get them whores to tote him. I bet they know how."

One of the whores, the one with a long scar down the side of her face, picked up the gold piece and tucked it in her bosom. Billy tipped his hat to her as he stepped over the dead man on his way out the door.

"I'm looking for Quick Billy Banks and by God, I'm gonna kill that son of a bitch!" Bunk Billings yelled as he hitched up his gun belt, slicked down his walrus mustache, and stuck out his fat gunt.

Billy had seen him before though he couldn't exactly recall the place. The man was so fat he could block out the sun. You weren't likely to forget a man that big.

"Where have we met? I can't remember the details," Billy said. He leaned back against the bar amiably and smiled at the fat man.

"That don't matter, because I'm about to kill you, you sonofab—"

Billy pulled his gun and the big man fell over dead, shot through the head. Billy scowled. Something didn't feel right. He wasn't a saint, and he had killed many men, but he didn't usually plug one that quick. The fatty had been going for his gun and his words had been threatening. Billy knew he wouldn't have any trouble from the decrepit old deputy that was serving as law these days. He was deaf as a post and usually drunk. Nobody in the Empress cared much either. They went back to their business as soon as the dust around the gargantuan's body settled.

"Dern it, Billy. He's awful big to carry out," Bob said.

Billy stared at him and he tried to get over the hinky feeling he had. Bob had said that before. Billy didn't respond. He tossed Bob a gold piece and flicked a second one at the group of whores who had taken an interest in the dead man. He grabbed a bottle of whiskey from the bar and headed out of the saloon, intent on drinking away the image of the angry fat man and the way he jiggled when he fell.

"He's too fat. I'll never get him out the door," Bob the bartender yelled. He kicked the corpse and watched it jiggle.

Billy pulled the Colt from its holster and shot Bob in the gut. Bob fell over screaming as blood poured from the hole in his stomach.

"Now you sure won't," Billy said. He laughed, mean and high-pitched. Everyone in the Empress looked away from him. He walked over to the fat man, ignoring Bob's cries, and shot the fat man a few more times for good measure. He knew the man's name was Bunk Billings before the tub of lard had ever opened his fat mouth. How he knew, Billy couldn't say, but when he had seen the man waddle through the door, he pulled his gun and shot him.

Billy wasn't a bit worried about the law. The deputy in this town was a drunken fool, and besides, they'd have to catch him first.

He nodded and smiled at the whore with the marked-up face. Her scar was long, red, and angry looking. No amount of time had seemed to heal it.

Billy pulled out two gold pieces and flung them at the whore. They hit her in the chest and fell to the floor. The whore stared at Billy, her face an unreadable mask. "Ma'am," Billy said, "I'll leave these two for you to sort out."

Billy avoided Bob's bloody, desperate grasp, stepped over the dead fatty, and rode out of town.

Billings never got the threat out of his mouth. Quick Billy Banks lived up to his name when he plugged the blustering fat man right between the eyes. He walked over to the body and stared at it a second, then he nodded, his face grim.

He walked back to the bar, swallowed the last of his whiskey, then shot Bob the Bartender in the head. He had to reload twice, but he was fast at that too. He killed almost everyone in the Empress. When he ran out of bullets, only a couple of the whores remained. The skinny one they called Beanpole screamed in the corner as she held her dead cowboy boyfriend. The one with the scarred up face sat calmly in a chair at the Faro table and watched. When Billy got to her, he put the Colt to her head and pulled the trigger six times. The whore didn't blink.

Billy nodded at her and tossed her a handful of gold coins.

Billy Banks started weeping as soon as the fat bastard stomped through the door to the Empress Saloon and yelled that he was, by God, going to kill him.

He wasn't sure if it was real or not. Was he awake or was he dreaming? Dream was the wrong word. It was more of a nightmare where every day that fat man burst through the door and demanded Billy's head.

Now Billy knew Bunk Billings well. He knew the wheeze of his voice as the fat man screamed, out of breath from the effort of carrying that much weight and rage around. The sound his hand made as it brushed his fat waist on its way to find the cheap pistol holstered around his massive bulk. He especially knew the thud Billings' body made every time it hit the wooden saloon floor.

Billy couldn't recall when he started to keep count of the number of times he shot the man. Once he became aware, he pulled out his knife and carved a notch in the bar for each time he killed old Bunk. He counted notch number three-hundred eighty six. He ran his fingers over the last notch as the tears streamed down his cheeks then turned around to face the man.

"I'm looking for Quick Billy Banks and by God, I'm gonna kill that son of a bitch!" Bunk Billings yelled as he hitched up his gun belt, slicked down his walrus mustache, and stuck out his fat gunt.

Billy walked up to him and pulled the gun from the man's holster. The fat man looked shocked. His eyes lost the anger they held and Billy saw the anger replaced by fear as Billy held the gun to his own head. He grabbed Bunk's chubby hand placed it on the gun. The fat man tried to jerk his hand away but Billy held it firm.

"Naw. You go ahead and shoot me then," Billy said.

"I-I… by God… I'll—" The fat man couldn't get the words out.

"I've heard you say it so many times, just do it. I'm tired and I can't no more," Billy sobbed.

Bunk Billings stared at Billy then looked around the saloon. He jerked his hand away and lost his balance. He tumbled to the floor with a solid thud. He landed on his back and rolled around a bit as he tried desperately to get to his feet. The sight was comical, like a turtle on its back, and Billy went from crying to laughing. He dropped the gun to floor and bent over laughing. He laughed until he was hiccupping and crying at the same time.

The rest of the saloon began to laugh too. They laughed at both men. The slapped the tables and pounded the floors as they whooped and hollered. Finally, Bunk Billings managed to roll over onto his side and stand up. He knocked over a few chairs then ran out the door as the crowd jeered at him.

Billy stood in the middle of the floor, laughing and crying. His shirtfront was wet from his slobber and snot. He couldn't believe the fat man was finally gone. He hadn't prayed since he was a boy in Georgia, at Sunday church with his mama, but he still remembered how. He dropped to his knees and thanked the Heavenly Father, Son, and the Holy Ghost for bringing it all to an end. He promised to stop gambling and killing people for money. He swore to never again steal, drink vile liquor, and Billy promised the Heavens above that he would never again engage a whore. He was right in the middle of promising to preach the Word from sea to sea and give up all Earthly pleasures when he felt the gun barrel press into his forehead. He opened his eyes to see the whore with the scar holding the gun.

She didn't smile as she pulled the trigger and Billy Banks' brains flew backward and splattered the bar and floor. His body hit the floor with a far less impressive thud than Bunk Billings had ever made, but he lay dead just the same.

The whore pulled Billy's wallet, fat with greenbacks, from his pocket and the purse full of gold coins from his vest. She walked over to the bar and set the gun down. Bob the Bartender poured her a glass of whiskey.

"Dern it, Vera, that was a long time to hold a grudge," he said.

Vera traced her scar. It was red and it still hurt even though Quick Billy Banks had cut her up ten years before. She downed the whiskey and nodded.

"Sure was," she said.

LUKA'S DESERT SCI-FI MOVIE

EXT. DESERT WASTELAND-DAY

The sun beats down on a figure lying on the rocky red sand. Hills can be seen in the distance, but the ground is flat and even. There are a few skeletal trees.

MOVING

A black military-style vehicle drives across the landscape. It makes no sound except the wheels on the rocky sand. It's powered by something other than gasoline.

The truck **STOPS** slowly when it approaches the figure. We can hear music playing muted inside the vehicle. It's Guns and Roses, Welcome to the Jungle. The music **BLARES** when the driver's side door opens.

A **TALL FIGURE** steps out. We can't tell if it's male or female. It's dressed in khaki desert fatigues that have a shiny look, like a barrier suit. It wears a helmet and mask that resemble an industrial full-face respirator with lighted filter cartridges on the sides. The mask is mirrored. We can't see inside.

A **SECOND FIGURE** exits from the passenger side of the vehicle. We can't tell if it's male or female either, but it's shorter than the driver.

Both regard the figure in the sand cautiously. The shorter one pulls an instrument from a pouch and holds it out.

. . .

TALL FIGURE (A FEMALE VOICE)

Well, is it dead or what?

SECOND FIGURE (A MALE VOICE)

Or what?

TALL FIGURE

Don't get cute, Daniels. Is it alive or dead?

Daniels punches a few buttons on the instrument and shakes his head.

DANIELS

I don't know. Something is up with the scope. Just getting noise.

He hits the scope a few times with his palm and shrugs.

DANIELS

We're blind. Your call, Jill.

. . .

JILL pauses and punches a few buttons on her wristband computer.

JILL

Base, this is Patrol Seven. We found somebody.

A MAN'S VOICE cuts in on the radio. It's fuzzy.

MAN'S VOICE

Gonna need more details than that, Jill.

JILL

Our scope is dead. Can't tell much without approaching.

The radio cuts in and out with static. Jill hits the radio a few times to clear the static but it does no good. She looks terrified and unsure of what to do.

JILL

Okay, too risky. Let's get back.

Daniels holds out his hand, questioning.

DANIELS

Looks like a kid Jill. Can't we at least check?

Jill shakes her head.

JILL

Negative. It's against protocol.

DANIELS

You've never been much for protocol. Look, cover me. I'll check.

JILL

No. Daniels. NO. I won't let you risk--

He puts his scope back in its pouch on his belt and pulls out a small cylinder. He flicks his wrist, and the cylinder elongates into a baton and hums.

. . .

DANIELS

I'll risk it. Just cover me. Anything happens, I give you full permission to ditch me.

JILL

I don't need your permission. Fucking idiot.

(She sighs and pulls out a small pistol. She trains it on the figure.)

JILL

GO. Hurry up.

Daniels nods. He approaches cautiously. The prone figure in the sand doesn't move. Daniels gets within the length of the baton. He uses it to poke the body. It doesn't move. He pokes it again and looks back at Jill.

DANIELS

Okay, I'm going to turn it over.

. . .

Jill nods and edges a bit closer to them. She trains her gun on the body and tenses as Daniels slowly bends down and grabs the body. He flips it over.

The body flops over and doesn't move. It's a **WOMAN**. She is bald, and her face is perfect. Young, unblemished. Not chapped or red as you might expect from exposure in the desert. She is wearing a clean white t-shirt and jeans, no shoes.

DANIELS

She's dead.

JILL

Something isn't right here.

Jill slowly walks closer but doesn't lower her gun. She looks around the area and sees a set of tracks.

DANIELS

Looks like she walked a long way. No signs of injury. She just fell over.

.   .   .

JILL

Let's go Daniels. We can't help and she doesn't have anything that can help us.

Daniels is searching the woman's body. He finds nothing.

DANIELS

Shouldn't we take the body back to the base? She's the first person we've seen since—

Daniels is cut off when the woman opens her eyes, sits up, and shoves her fist through his chest. He gurgles and goes limp. The woman removes her fist from his body and turns to Jill.

Jill fires six shots directly into the woman's chest. There is no blood, and the woman doesn't move. She absorbs the energy of the bullets and stands up. She advances on Jill.

.   .   .

Jill pulls out her baton and flicks it to life. The woman is close now and Jill shoves the energy baton into the woman's stomach. The baton crackles and hisses as it sends electrical energy into the woman. It stops her momentarily, and she twitches quickly, faster than any human can move.

Jill stares.

Jill tries to call someone on her comm, but the comm signal is just loud static.

The woman smiles. She grabs Jill's baton and easily pulls it away. She shoves it into Jill's chest and pushes the power button.

Jill screams and spasms, then collapses on the sand. The comm signal is still static.

The woman gives a few more twitches as the last of the electrical energy is absorbed. She looks down at her chest. The bullet holes are being repaired by tiny black tendrils that shoot out of the holes, fill in her synthetic flesh, and recede back into her body. The woman kneels down and removes Jill's respirator mask. Jill's face is frozen in a grimace and her eyes are bloody and bulging.

The woman looks at Jill quizzically for a few seconds. Tiny black tendrils emerge from her scalp. They pull hair out--hair that matches Jill's red locks. The tendrils shoot out all over her face and change her to be an exact copy of Jill. The woman undresses Jill and disrobes. She puts on Jill's suit, all but the mask.

She walks over to Daniels and places her palm flat over his chest. The black tendrils shoot out and repair his skin and his suit. They seem to eat all the blood and when they are done, Daniels is whole, but dead. She smashes his respirator mask, then loads him into the back of the vehicle.

She holds up the comm on her wrist and the static clears.

· · ·

THE WOMAN (IN JILL'S VOICE)

Base, I'm on my way back. Have medical prepped. Daniels had an accident.

RADIO

Damn it Jill, what happened? What happened to the person?

THE WOMAN

Respirator cracked. Freak thing. She was dead. I'm on my way.

RADIO (DEFEATED SOUNDING)

Roger that. Safely Jill. Come back safely.

The woman smiles. She dons the respirator mask and helmet. The music is still blaring as she climbs in the vehicle. She doesn't touch any buttons but the music changes from the hard rock to 80's New Wave. New Order's Blue Monday blares from the speakers. She shuts the door and turns the vehicle back in the direction it came.

. . .

FADE OUT on the vehicle disappearing over the horizon while the music plays.

COTTON LOVE

Ext. Suburban Neighbourhood- Stormy Night

We travel through the air, closing in on a two-story house. The motion stops in a nest in the corner of a rain gutter on the second story. **VICTORIA**, a female bird, is tucked into the corner of the nest, shivering.

CAMERA PANS OUT, revealing that we have been following **ANDY**, a male bird, who is now in the nest facing Victoria.

. . .

ANDY

Oh, my dear, sweet Victoria.

VICTORIA

Ah, fuck off, will you, Andy? I've no time for your randiness today. It's blowin' a bloody gale out 'ere.

ANDY

'Tis the heavens above, flapping its wings to soar with the heights of your beauty.

Andy spreads his wings and turns, shaking his colourful booty feathers at Victoria. He struts, cooing sweet nothings to his intended.

VICTORIA

(Rolls eyes and sighs)
Andy. Fer Fuck sakes. Pitch yer woo in some other shithole. I's jus' tryin' to stay alive out 'ere.

ANDY smiles and changes his tactics. He fishes around inside his feathers, pulling out a shiny piece of tinfoil and setting it in front of VICTORIA. Victoria at the foil, then up at Andy, and shrugs.

VICTORIA

What of it?

ANDY

Isn't it splendid?

VICTORIA

Well, no, not really-

ANDY

It shines quite like the moon shines just for you. If you look at it, it will reflect the most beautiful image back to you

VICTORIA

Bloody hell...

.   .   .

Victoria turns her back to Andy and drives her face into the nest.

Andy scowls, looking both defeated and puzzled. Lightning flashes, striking a nearby tree, followed by a deafening crack of thunder. Victoria screams and rushes over to Andy. Andy also shrieks, wrapping his wings around Victoria. They huddle together, hiding from the storm.

EXT. SUBURBAN NEIGHBOURHOOD-DAY

We follow the same spiral, leading to the nest in the rain gutter, though now the nest is in a state of disrepair. There is not much left other than some sticks and soggy grass and papers holding the nest together. Victoria is in the nest, trying to salvage what she can of her home.

Andy has returned to the nest, a bundle of sticks in his beak. He sets them next to Victoria.

.   .   .

VICTORIA

Seriously?

ANDY

I'm only trying to help.

VICTORIA

Only tryin' to help, are ya?

Victoria swipes her wing across the pile of sticks Andy has brought her, knocking them out of the nest to the ground below.

VICTORIA

What you are tryin' to do is trick your way into my favour. You want a lover, and yer using this tragedy to get what ye' dude parts desires!

Andy looks sad, then he smiles.

ANDY

You're just stressed, my ethereal darling. I can see the strain, feel your melancholy. My dude parts are not what aches for you. It's my soul that craves your happiness, your beauty, your presence. I adore you, fair Victoria. I would be honoured to bask in your presence, and bring light to your life.

Victoria stares at Andy, then bursts out laughing.

VICTORIA
(wiping away tears of laughter)
You bloody wanking fool. You're too much. Git yer lame ass outta my mess of a nest.

Victoria turns her back to Andy and keeps pecking away at her repairs in a futile attempt to fill the holes.

EXT. SUBURBAN NEIGHBORHOOD-NIGHT

It is a clear night. We following the camera as it once again flies into the nest. We find Victoria hunched in the corner of the rain gutter, shivering, only a few broken sticks scattered around her, remnants of her old nest. She is crying. ANDY steps over to her and wraps his wing over her.

ANDY

My love. All will be well, I assure you.

VICTORIA

Ah, go eat a fuck, you twatting bugger.

ANDY

I shan't. I shan't eat a fuck. What I will do is stop bothering you with trite offerings, and give you something truly divine; a gift worthy of the queen you are.

Victoria bangs her head agains the rain gutter, and shuffles out from beneath Andy's wing.

VICTORIA

Excuse me while I jump from this gutter and fail to break my fall with flight.

. . .

ANDY

Hear me out, my love.

Victoria, clearly exasperated, stares at Andy for a moment, then nods.

ANDY

I must show you. Follow me.

Andy hops to the edge of the gutter and on to the shingles on the second story of the house. Victoria hesitates, but follows. They hop up to the peak of the house, and Andy starts down the other side.

VICTORIA

(Whispering)

Andy, you fool! What are you doing? What about the beast?

Andy and Victoria look down into the yard below. There is a pool, with a massive, grey dog laying on the deck on its back, legs splayed open.

. . .

ANDY

Unless the beast sprouts wings, she does not have the means to cause us any bother.

Andy looks down at the dog, and cocks a brow.

ANDY

Or the energy, it would seem.

The dog farts, then keeps snoring.

Victoria nods in agreement.

Andy keeps hopping along the peak of the house until he reaches the edge, then waves Victoria over with his wing.

ANDY

Here, my soulmate. Under this peak. Beneath this loose material.

Andy pulls back the siding with his beak, revealing a hole. He holds it open and tilts his head, motioning for Victoria to go in the hole. She does, and he follows behind.

INT. INSIDE THE ATTIC

Victoria gasps. The Attic is cluttered with moving boxes and instrument cases, and mountains of sundries stocked up from Costco. Andy flaps his wings and ascends to a space along the roof with about 20 centimeters of clearance. Victoria follows, and finds a hidden hole about a square meter in size. In the corner is a fluffy white nest.

VICTORIA
(hopping over and pulling at the nest)
What in tarnation?

. . .

ANDY

Your new home, my love. Fit for a Queen.

VICTORIA

But how did you-

ANDY

The supplies are plenty inside: Paper for the wiping of thine human booties, threads from their flesh covers, and...

Andy pulls a white piece of cotton from the nest

ANDY

... A grande supply of Q-tips, dissembled and arranged into your quarters, m'lady.

Victoria settles into the nest, sinking into the cloud of cotton.

VICTORIA

This is all... You pulled this all off... Q-Tips? That must have taken forever! It's so much work! It's-

Andy hops to her and places a wing over her beak to quiet her.

ANDY

It's no more than you deserve. You deserve the world, my love, and I intend to give it to you on a silver platter.

Andy tucks his beak under his wing and pulls out a ring: A Q-tip bent into a ring, the cotton tip wrapped in silver foil. He slides the ring onto Victoria's leg.

ANDY

Victoria, will you-

Victoria looks at the ring on her leg. She jumps up, chirping and chattering, and wraps her wings around Andy, rubbing her head against his.

· · ·

VICTORIA

Yes! All the yesses in the world, my love!

The camera pans out as the betrothed embrace, the light shining off the foil of the ring. Pachelbel's Canon in D plays, the volume a steady crescendo.

FADE OUT

HOW MAGGIE GOT HER GROOVE BACK

"Another, Maggie?" the bartender asked as he held up the bottle of Canadian Club whiskey. The air was thick with smoke from cheap cigarettes, the smell of which was burned so deeply into the walls and furniture that had the whole place caught fire, it would have burnt and smelled just like a pack of Marlboros.

Maggie looked up, her eyes glassy and red from the whiskey and smoke. She nodded and exhaled a plume of smoke of her own, adding it to the perpetual cloud. The bartender poured her a generous slug of liquor, capped the bottle, and returned it to the shelf. He smiled politely at Maggie and headed down to the other end of the bar where two old men were watching the Wheel of Fortune on the television and playing pull tab tickets. He kept a watchful eye on Maggie, sure to keep her glass topped off, but he kept his distance.

Maggie picked up the glass and took a swig. It was terrible stuff, and it burned unpleasantly all the way down her gullet, but it did its job well enough—as well as the top shelf stuff did—at the right price. It took the edge off her hunger. If she'd had a meal in the preceding few days, it would ease it entirely. If she hadn't eaten, it would lessen the stabbing, twisting feeling in the pit of her stomach, but it would never truly be gone.

Tonight was that night. She hadn't eaten in two weeks, and the gnawing she felt in her stomach was almost unbearable. Five drinks had barely taken the edge off. It wasn't that she lacked meals, they were easy enough to come by, she simply didn't feel like eating. It was funny to her that she could feel that way, painfully hungry, like there was a rat eating at her insides, and yet indifferent. She knew that she needed to eat; she wasn't suicidal, it was just that she was tired of the act. When she had been young, the hunger and desire mixed all together in glorious, radiant waves. She would tear and rip and gorge herself on fat and flesh and blood until she couldn't move. It had been so easy then, so simple. She was hungry, and she wanted, so she took and she ate. She had enjoyed the sport then. Attracting. Ensnaring. Tempting them with the promise of ecstasy then watching the rapture turn to horror when she showed them what she really was. At first that had been better than the meal. Seeing the fear and panic on their faces had satisfied something deep inside her, deeper than the hunger, something basic and nasty and beautiful.

She had no idea how long it took for all that to wear thin. It wasn't an epiphanic moment. She couldn't pinpoint one specific time or place when she had realized there was no point. It had come to her gradually, each meal less delicious, less satisfying than the last until finally the taste of flesh and blood wasn't discernable to her any longer. It was nutritional matter to be consumed. If sawdust would have sated her hunger, she would have been equally as amenable to eating it.

The men bored her. They were all the same—panting, needful—they disgusted her. In the beginning, she remembered feeling desired and powerful, and sometimes, on the rarest occasion, loved. Now she felt empty and alone, and sometimes, on most occasions, contemptuous.

This bar was as good as any other she had ever found. The men that came in were unremarkable and mundane. Some were transients, truckers, travelers. Some were something else. None of them would be missed. Even if the occasional family man did wander in, if he was patronizing this bar with its cheap, watered-down liquor and smoke-ruined interior, he couldn't have been high quality. His family would collect insurance money if there was any to collect, or they would be rid of him, so Maggie didn't care.

She ran her hand down her prosthetic leg. It didn't fit her well because she had lost weight. Her stump slid around in the harness and made squishing noises when she walked. ThHeer stump had never healed. It was a mess of ancient stitches and pus. She still recalled the day her mother sawed the leg off and fed it to the fire. She had burned like the flesh as the flames consumed her soul, leaving a void and hunger, and a perpetually festering wound. It could be smelled at great distances so she always took care to cover the rotten smell with rose water. Admittedly, it didn't smell good, she could never cover the odor of rot completely, but the rose smell complemented and transformed it into some-thing that made them wonder until she could glamour them. Once she cast her spell, the smell of a hundred festering wounds wouldn't have made them leave.

Her leg ached, and she winced as her stomach twisted and growled. It was audible, and the bartender looked alarmed at the other end of the bar. Maggie took a long swallow of her whiskey. She couldn't feel the burn any longer and that made her sigh. She was as numb to the pain and indifference as she was going to get for the evening. The bar was empty save the bartender and the two crusty old sods at the end. None of them were of interest to her. She was about to pack it in when the door opened.

The young man that walked through the door was tall and tanned. His perfectly sculpted body was on display through his designer polo shirt and his jeans hugged every inch of his lower half. She could smell him from across the room. His cologne smelled expensive, and the old men coughed a bit as they caught a whiff of it. The fact that their cigarette smoke-ruined noses could smell him at all, let alone be choked by it, spoke volumes about the veracity of his smell.

He looked around the room and scowled, but when he saw Maggie, his face lit up in a smile. Maggie knew that smile well. It wasn't exactly happy, more predatory and mean. He adjusted himself confidently, swaggered over, and sat down on the bar stool next to her.

"Mind if I sit here?" he asked with a wink and roguish grin.

"Makes no difference to me," Maggie replied. She stubbed out her cigarette and pulled another one from the pack.

"Allow me," he said as he took the cheap Bic lighter from her, held it up, and struck the wheel to light it. He held it out for her.

She stared at him for a second, then rolled her eyes

and leaned in toward him to light the cigarette. She puffed a few times, then leaned back and regarded him more closely.

It was a gesture from another time, and one that was much more suave with a Zippo. His sandy blond hair was gelled to perfection, and when he smiled, his white teeth glistened and twinkled in the low light. He couldn't have been more than twenty-one. Maggie was an excellent judge of age. She would know exactly how old he was if she tasted him. She cocked her head and looked at him, then sniffed deeply. She narrowed her eyes. There was something else, a different smell that was barely there, buried beneath the waves of Calvin Klein's Eternity that wafted from him every time he moved. She thought she had smelled it before, but it had been so long ago that she couldn't place it.

She sucked in a lung-full of smoke then blew it out at him as she studied him. "Thanks," she said.

"Anything for a lady," he said. He motioned toward her drink. "What are you drinking?"

"Canadian Club," she said.

"Interesting," he said.

"Is it?" Maggie asked.

"I think that it is." He motioned for the bartender. "I'll have what the lady is having," he said.

"For real?" the bartender asked, eyeing them both warily.

"That's what I said, didn't I?"

The bartender shrugged as he pulled the Canadian Club down from the top shelf where it didn't belong. He poured another drink for Maggie and filled a tumbler marked by dust and greasy fingerprints for the young man. He pocketed the crisp twenty-dollar bill and went back to his position at the other end of the bar.

"He's interesting," the young man said.

"No, he isn't," Maggie said. She sipped her drink and stared ahead. What was that smell? She really wanted to know, and it was right there, in the back of her brain, but the whiskey had dulled her senses just enough so that she couldn't remember.

"What brings you to such a fine establishment as this?" he asked. She almost laughed as he took a drink of the cheap liquor and grimaced.

"I'm drinking," she said.

"Alone? That's a real shame," he said. He winked at her. "Fortuitous of me to wander in here."

"Is it?" Maggie asked.

"Oh, I think so," he said. "I certainly wasn't expecting to meet such a beautiful woman in a place like this."

"Weren't you now?" she asked. What was he doing? He didn't sound like a young man. He looked the part, perfect and sculpted, but he didn't sound it.

She had known many young men—she was an expert —but she couldn't recall ever meeting one quite like him. Or could she? She sniffed him again, and her stomach growled.

"May I ask the lady for her name?"

"Maggie," she said.

"Maggie… I think I'm in love," he said.

"Are you now?" she asked. Her stomach growled again.

"You have beautiful eyes," he said. He stared deeply into hers and smiled. "Beautiful…"

She was old and she was tired. When she glamoured herself, she was barely able to pass for forty these days. It worked on the dried-up old men that came in there, but no way should it work on a young man. And anyway, she hadn't bothered much with the glamour yet.

"My name is Channing," he said.

"No, it isn't," Maggie laughed.

"It is," he grinned and nudged her good leg with his. "Why would I lie?" He reached over and patted her leg.

She looked down at his hand, which he hadn't removed, then she looked up at him. She concentrated and focused the full might of her glamour on him. She could see it in their eyes when it hit them and she had them. They turned glassy. His eyes were clear.

"What are you?" Maggie asked.

He leaned in close, his lips brushing against her ear. "All yours," he whispered. "Is there someplace we can go?"

She was curious, that was all, she told herself. Her spells always worked. Always. But here he was, propositioning her, which was her thing, and she hadn't bewitched him at all. He moved his hand higher up her thigh and left it there.

"Sure," she said. The effects of the Canadian Club were gone, and she felt the gnawing hunger return. It made her breath catch in her throat, which he mistook for something else. His hand flexed and he breathed heavily in her ear. She stood up and adjusted her leg, then took him by the hand and led him down the hallway to the back door. When they got outside, he pushed her against the grimy brick wall. Tall weeds overran the area around them and night things rustled in the grass. He paid no attention to any of it as he pressed himself against her. His kiss was amateur and greedy, which was the first thing he had done that reminded her of a young man. He lingered too long on her lower lip, and when he moved away and lower to shove his face in her breasts, she finally realized what the smell was. The crisp night air diffused his cologne and she caught the whiff of Sulphur.

She growled and shoved him away.

"What are you?"

"What? I'm…" He looked ridiculous, standing there with his fly open and an exaggerated erection. She had seen every possible size and shape, and his belonged to a horse, not a man.

"Really? Don't you think that's a bit much?" She pointed to his cock.

"I don't know what you mean," he said.

"Cut the shit. What are you?"

"Cut the shit yourself," he said. "What are *you*? I threw enough at you tonight for a hundred women."

"Not a woman. Not for a very long time," Maggie said. "Show me what you really are, and I'll show you," Maggie said.

"On three," he said.

Maggie nodded. "One… two… three."

She dropped every bit of magic that she had. Her clothes dissolved away, and she stood there, naked, wrinkled elongated breasts dangling from her chest. Her stomach was a mass of stretch marks and fat rolls that drooped and folded at odd angles. Her stubbed thigh was green and black with oozing yellow pus dripping from the perpetual wound. Her eyes went from warm brown to mean black nuggets of coal and her skin was mottled with brown age spots.

At the same time, he shook and shimmied. His clothing burned off his body, leaving the heavy smell of Sulphur in the air. His gigantic cock shriveled into a thin, pathetic worm attached to sad, sagging balls. His perfect body melted away into ancient folds of flesh marked with blisters and sores. Wild white hair sprouted from his nose and ears. He stared at her with yellow eyes and his green forked tongue snaked out and tasted the air.

"Oh," he said. "I didn't know."

"This is my place," she snarled.

"Calm down. I said I didn't know," he said. "I was only hungry."

"This is where I eat," Maggie said. "You find your own place."

"You'll starve in there," he said. "When I saw you, I couldn't believe my luck. There's nobody else in there. Is there ever?"

"Sometimes," Maggie sighed. "I don't eat much anymore."

"Me either," he said. "I know I have to, but…"

Maggie nodded. "I know. It doesn't matter anymore."

"It really doesn't," he agreed. "I didn't mean to overstep."

Maggie looked at him and shrugged. She made a minimal effort and glamoured herself presentable. He shook again and regained his young form. They went back inside. Maggie heaved herself up onto her bar stool. He sat down beside her and sipped his whiskey.

"This stuff is awful."

Maggie drank all of hers and smiled. "Nobody is pouring it down your throat." She pulled a cigarette from her pack and waited for him to light it for her.

They sat in comfortable silence as they listened to each other's stomachs growl. They were both starving.

THE DOWNFALL OF WINNIFRED
BEISSNER

Winnifred Beissner was an insatiable cunt.

And everyone knew it, too.

Wherever she went she left behind a trail of misery, ranging from minor irritation to outright despair and hatred. From criticizing one's taste in food and wine, to the make of their vehicles and the desirability of one's pets, she spared no expense at wriggling into every nook and cranny of people's lives to make them miserable and leave them reeling when she made her departure. If she made her departure. She had a nasty habit of inserting herself into people's lives and living there like a virus beneath the skin, subtle but festering, waiting to flair up and reek havoc for her own entertainment.

The thing about Winnifred was that she, herself,

had no idea how unpalatable she was. She was perfect, you see, from her culinary skills to her sexual prowess. She blew through lives like a hurricane, then acted surprised when the wind rustled her own hair. She wanted everyone to like her—love her, rather—but reveled in the chaos she left in her wake.

She seemed unstoppable, this beast, a demon with pink-streaked hair, but her time had come. Her demise came at the fingertips an old acquaintance, who she stumbled upon by happenstance.

Judith Maney.

"Well oh my stars, will you look at this?"

Winnifred's voice was shrill, and dozens of eyes in the small diner squeezed tight in repulsion at the sound.

"Winnifred?"

"Why yes, silly! Well if it isn't ol' Judith Maney, in the flesh."

Judith forced the corners of her mouth into a pained smile.

"And I must say, you've plenty of it," Winnifred said, winking.

Judith cocked her head, confused.

"Flesh, my dear. Put on a few pounds since we last saw each other, haven't you?"

A booming chortle released from Winnifred's

throat as she slapped Judith on the love handles, jiggling her body.

"Oh yes, you're Ricky's wife, aren't you?" Judith said.

Like she had been slapped, Winnifred's face contorted and her hand flew to her mouth.

"Oh for heaven's sake, no! That oaf?"

Judith's brow furrowed in confusion. "I'm sorry, I just—"

"We've divorced. That man has problems, Judith. Absolutely out-of-control drinking, gambling, philandering. Can't tolerate that kind of business."

"Suppose not." Judith shot a glance to the barista, who shrugged and smirked.

"So are you going to invite me to dinner?" Winnifred said.

The barista brought over Judith's coffee, and Winnifred snatched it off the counter and slung her massive pewter handbag over her shoulder.

"Come now, let's walk. You parked close?" Winnifred cawed.

"Uh, yes, but—"

"I can ride with you. I'll hang out for the afternoon and have dinner, then Uber it back here to my car." Winnifred winked. "I want to let you have some wine, so you don't need to drive me back."

Without giving Judith a chance to argue, Winnifred was out the door. Judith followed.

"Huh."

"What?" Judith said, looking back at Winnifred as they walked into Judith's modest two story home.

Winnifred had done nothing but complain on the drive over, criticizing Judith's simple Chevy and the downtrodden appearance of the neighborhood. That is to say the neighborhood had children playing, their toys strewn about, and neighbours congregating in the street.

"A touch exhibitionist, isn't it?" Winnifred had said.

They don't have their dicks and tits out, you twatting wretch!

Judith's patience had grown onion-skin thin on the long drive home. And now that they were inside it seemed that Winnifred had more to say.

"Oh nothing," Winnifred said, her nose in the air. "I just prefer real flagstone and hardwood over…" Winnifred waved a hand over the main living space and adjacent kitchen, "… this."

Deep breath.

"Suits us just fine," Judith said. "It's tough, with Thomas and the pets."

"Huh."

The issue was dropped, but Judith could see Winnifred's eyes assessing everything.

Why is she here?

"Can I get you something to drink, Winnie?"

Winnifred huffed. "It's Winnifred, if you please."

Teeth clenched. "Of course. Winnifred. Can I offer you a beverage?"

"Wine, please."

"Red or white?"

"White, of course. Look at the time, dear!"

Judith bit her tongue. "Of course. Coming right up."

Judith went in the kitchen and put her hands on the counter, closing her eyes and taking a few deep, calculated, calming breaths.

Don't let her get to you. This is fine. This is nothing. A quick visit, then she'll be gone.

A rustling from the other room drew Judith's attention. She selected a bottle of chardonnay from the fridge and poured a modest glass—not too full but still generous—and went back to the living room. Winnifred was there, rearranging the ornaments on the mantle. She noticed Judith there, but didn't stop.

"Looks better this way, don't you think?"

"Here's your wine, Winnifred."

After taking the glass and sniffing it, Winnifred took a dainty sip and swished it around her mouth.

"Huh."

"You don't like it?"

"It's… what is it?"

"Chardonnay."

"Yes dear, but what region? Price range? What winery?"

"Uh, Kroger's wine of the week."

"Yep," Winnifred laughed, handing the glass back. "Not for actual wine drinkers, but appealing to the masses. A spikey fruit juice, if you will."

Judith eyed the wine and looked back at Winnifred.

"I don't know what to offer you."

"I'll help myself," Winnifred said, breezing past Judith into the kitchen.

Judith looked at the glass in her hand and downed the entire thing in three hefty gulps.

The final two hours of the afternoon were uneventful. Winnifred talked about Winnifred—where she was volunteering now that she was retired, who she had been fucking since throwing her useless husband to the curb, how good she was at this, that, and the other thing. Judith wondered if Winnifred remembered anything about her, anything at all. It had been a good decade since they'd seen each other, and lots had changed. Judith had met Jim, and they had Thomas, who was now a lanky teenager with aspirations of Berkley. They had made themselves a quaint little life, her as a graphic designer and Jim as an accountant. All was good.

But not according to Winnifred.

"So you make flyers?" Winnifred said, sipping on her wine with a scowl on her face.

"Not exactly. I help marketing firms with visual graphics—"

"I can paint," Winnifred interrupted with a raised voice and swoop of her hand. "Like, really paint, brushes and oils and such. Not this playing around on computers, video games and such. Dying art, it is. Anyone with a tablet and a phone thinks they're a creative genius."

Judith opened her mouth to reply, but the front door swung open and in came Thomas, backpack over his shoulder and manilla envelope in hand.

"Hey honey," Judith said, jumping up and giving her son a hug. "How was school?"

"Meh," he said, brushing his hair out of his eyes. "But I did get that job down at the pet store. Weekends, and I get discounts."

"Saving for the snake?" Judith asked.

"Yep. And my Ford Raptor."

"Ah, a man with good taste in vehicles!" Winnifred

said, jumping off the couch. When she placed her hand on Judith's arm, encasing it like talons on prey, Judith winced. So did Thomas. "Now shoo, young man. Your mother and I haven't seen each other in a long time, and we are trying to catch up. Have you no friends to go hang out with."

Thomas stared at the mess that was Winnifred, then tilted his head at his mom.

"Not yet, sweetheart."

"Okay," Thomas said, saluting Winnifred. "Later."

And with that, Thomas bounded up the stairs in three long leaps, disappearing behind his bedroom door. A moment later, his music came on, soft, but loud enough to be heard from the floor below.

And just loud enough to drown her out.

"Huh."

"Huh?"

"Suppose not all kids have manners. I'm used to dealing with normal kids."

Judith's hands clenched into fists as Winnifred turned and walked back towards the kitchen.

"Let's get cooking, shall we?"

"Yes. Let's."

And get tonight over with.

"Honey! I'm home!"

Jim came into the kitchen and dropped his briefcase on the counter.

"What's this? Winnifred Beissner? I mean, how long has it been?"

"Too long," Winnifred said, sidling up to Jim and giving him a kiss on the cheek. He wrapped an arm around her and gave her hair a tousle.

"What have you been up to? Why are you here?"

We are all wondering that, Judith thought.

"I ran into Judy downtown at the coffee shop, thought we'd have a dinner date. Isn't it lovely?"

"Judith."

Winnifred paused, her smile frozen but waning ever so slightly.

"Pardon me?"

"Judith. My name is Judith."

Winnifred's lips formed a tight line as her eyes regarded both Judith and Jim. "Very well. I never know what to call you, but if that's what you prefer—"

"What's cookin'?" Jim asked.

He wasn't a confrontational fellow, and Judith was sure he could feel the tension hanging thick in the air.

"I'm preparing a classic Thai dish. You guys will be amazed at what a proper meal tastes like."

"Indeed," Jim said. "I'm going to change. Be back in a jiffy."

After Jim had left the room, Winnifred rinsed her hands in the sink and headed to the hall.

"I'm going to relieve myself, Judy. Mind you stir the shrimp, okay? And not with that awful wooden spoon. Use the bamboo one."

Judith nodded, for fear if she answered verbally she might end up telling Winnifred how to season and eat a fuck.

The table was set, and dinner plated by the time Winnifred and Jim arrived back in the kitchen.

"You okay" Judith asked. "You were gone a while."

"Yes, well, I had to freshen up my makeup."

"You look fine, my dear," Jim said, giving Winnifred's hair another tousle. "We're all casual here, anyways.

Dinner was delicious—Winnifred really could cook —but the conversation was less appealing, another rehashing of everything Winnifred was and everyone else wasn't. Even Jim seemed to tire of the conversation, his eyes growing distant, and his attention to eating far more intense than need be.

"Hey, where's Tommy?" Jim asked.

"In his room," Judith said, and a smile sprouted across her face. "He got the job.

"Well that's wonderful!"

"Now maybe he could look at getting some manners."

Judith and Jim stopped chewing and started at Winnifred.

"Like I told Judith, I'm used to dealing with normal kids, but your boy, wooo!"

Jim looked at Judith. "Something happen?"

"Winnifred happened."

Jim looked at Judith, his eyes searching her.

"Not yet," Judith said, patting Jim's hand.

Daggers could have flown from Winnifred's eyes with the sharpness of her glare. "What ever does that mean?"

Another deep breath. "Nothing. This Thai is really good, by the way."

After a brief pause, Judith suspected Winifred was deciding whether to engage or not, Winifred cracked a toothy smile. "Well, I season well, like I was raised. Would be a whole lot better if I'd had decent ingredients to work with."

Judith wondered, thorough the remainder of the meal and a handful more of Winnifred stories, who's teeth were grinding harder when they chewed: hers or Jim's?

As soon as the last morsel was consumed, Jim disappeared into his study and shut the door. Judith was surprised he lasted as long as he had, his tolerance for bullshit and assholes being minimal at best.

She and Winnifred cleaned up the table then tackled the dishes, Judith washing and Winnifred at her hip, drying.

"It's terrible, you know. Him expecting you to serve him like that."

"What?"

"Jim. Comes home, expects dinner, doesn't help clean up."

"He helps."

"Not that I see."

"You've been here once. In ever."

"Be that as it may, this looks like routine for you."

"What it actually is is none of your business."

Lips a tight line again, Winnifred dried the dishes with more force. "You don't need to get defensive. For someone who has recently suffered a divorce, you should heed my warning and warmly welcome my advice."

Judith rolled her eyes. "I assure you my marriage is rock solid."

"Is it?" Winnifred said, placing the dish she was drying down on the counter.

Judith didn't respond, but she did stop washing and turned to face Winnifred.

"How's your sex life?"

"None of your damn business."

"That bad, huh." Winnifred laughed. "Not surprising, the way he was all over me and ignored you. The way he criticizes you around guests." Winnifred tapped a bony finger on Judith's chest. "You're better that that, girl. Toughen up, stand up for yourself."

To avoid punching a bitch in the throat, Judith set down the sponge and excused herself. She went down the hall to the guest bathroom and locked herself inside, leaning her head against the back of the door and closing her eyes.

No. It's not that bad. She'll be gone soon. I can last.

When she opened her eyes and turned around, she wasn't so sure anymore.

Judith's make-up—expensive eyeliner and nail polish, highlighter and lip stain—was strewn across the counter, lids off, makeup spilled on the counter. A new makeup brush was removed from its package and coated in powder, and her hairbrush was in the sink. Upon closer inspection Judith found strands of neon pink hair tangled in the bristles…

Enough was enough.

Judith marched back to the kitchen, rehearsing in

her head what she would say to evict her unwanted guest. When she walked in, however, the kitchen was empty, save a rack full of wet dishes, the dishtowel tossed on the counter beside.

Where the fuck did she go?

"Thomas?"

With a sinking feeling in her gut, Judith hopped up the stairs, two at a time, and banged on Thomas' door.

"You okay?" Judith said.

The door opened.

"Yeah, Mom, what's up?"

Judith looked down the hall.

"You hear anyone come up here?"

"Your guest?" Thomas said, eyebrow raised.

"Anyone."

"Nope. But my music—"

Judith barreled down the stairs towards Jim's office. As she approached the door, she heard that shrill, grating voice. Judith quieted her steps, slowly creeping until her ear was pressed against the door.

"You are insane," Jim said, clearly agitated.

"You are such a strong, handsome man," Winnifred cooed.

A shuffle on the desk, a gasp.

"What in the actual fuck are you doing, woman?"

"What she won't, I imagine."

Judith burst through the door. Jim was stumbling

back from the desk, hands over his eyes, face scrunched in anger or disgust, she couldn't tell. Maybe both.

And there. On the floor. Winnifred's slacks and hot pink thong crumpled in a pile. And Winifred, on Jim's desk, legs spread and fingers buried deep inside herself.

"Fantastic," Judith said, walking around to where Jim had squeezed himself in by the window.

"You like it?" Winnifred said, stroking herself. "Waxed yesterday, on the off chance I might see some acquaintances I could get together with."

"Yep, looks quite… prepubescent," Judith said, staring at the light reflecting off Winnifred's smooth, shiny business.

Jim looked at Judith.

Judith looked at Jim.

Thomas had come to the door, looking at all three of them.

"Mom?"

"Judith?"

Judith nodded.

"It's time."

Winnifred slid off the desk and pulled on her clothes.

"Time for what?" she said as she fussed with her coif. "Dessert? A snifter of Brandy? Didn't think you people had it in you. Moonshine, maybe."

She laughed, the sound a thousand nails piercing Judith's skull.

"Come, Winnie," Judith said as she left the office.

Winnifred followed with Jim close on her tail. They all snaked into the dining room where Judith took her place at the head of the table. Jim pulled out a chair, motioning for Winnifred to sit.

"Well, what a gentleman," she cackled, touching his bicep. "I think someone might be coming around to my," she pointed at her clothed, bald snatch, "honey pot."

"Mom?" Tommy said, shifting uncomfortably.

"Yes, dear. Please."

"What's going on?" Winnifred asked, not looking in the least bit concerned.

"I told you, Winnifred, Judith said as she cut into the cheesecake under glass on the table. "Not that you listened. You haven't stopped talking about yourself for one, fucking, goddamn moment."

The air sucked out of the room as Judith slammed the knife through the cake, punctuating every word.

"You. Are. A. Fucking, Trainwreck."

Winnifred balled her fists. "Pardon me, you wench?!"

"You gloat, you lie, you steal, you cheat. Everyone knows it. You've tried to ride every husband, be besties with every wife. Criticize every home, car, child, possession. You must be the best, the most coveted, the center of the," chop, "fucking," chop, "universe."

"I won't stand to be attacked like this."

"Can dish it but can't take it, eh Winnifred?"

Judith placed a piece of cake on her plate, the plate in front of Jim, and a plate for Tommy.

"You think we just happened upon me at that coffee shop Winnifred? After all these years, you think that we just randomly stumbled into each other?"

A pour of chocolate syrup, a dollop of whipped cream.

"I was the only one from our class whose life you hadn't plowed through yet."

A garnish of cherries.

"But my life has something everyone else's doesn't, Winnifred."

She was shaking now, her lower lip quivering, her eyes wet.

"But do you hate me? Are we still friends?" Winifred mewled.

Judith leaned back and scooped a hefty piece of cheesecake in her mouth.

"Winnifred, have you met my pets? I don't think you've been introduced.

With a nod, Tommy opened the door to the basement.

In a flurry of snappy teeth and greasy fur, dozen

upon dozens of giant rats swarmed into the kitchen from the basement, coating Winnifred like oil. The more she screamed, the more they ate with vigor, terrain flesh and swallowing fat and tendons in great globs. Some weren't hungry, they just tore off hunks of flesh as tossed in to the side. Blood splattered all over the kitchen as Winnifred tried to fight, flailing and screeching like a wounded banshee. Finally, the rats gnawed through her trachea, releasing a geyser of blood that ended her reign of terror.

Jim took a bite of cheesecake.

"You lasted longer than I thought you would," he said, watching the rats pick Winnifred's bones clean, two of them suckling at her jellied eyeballs.

"I'm surprised, too."

Thomas stepped gingerly over the corpse, that was gyrating with fat and flatulent rats, and took a seat at the table.

"Ah, cheesecake! My favorite."

Judith smiled and raised a glass of Chardonnay to the Downfall of Winnifred Beissner.

THE LAST NINE SECONDS

"To your right, Bill, 10 degrees." The radio crackled with static, cut out, then came back. "You see it?"

Bill looked through the viewer, then turned the periscope handles precisely ten degrees. A man with an orange backpack was sitting against the side of the dry-cleaning shop, right up against the big picture window advertising same day service and wash and fold by the pound. He was so still he might have been mistaken for a mannequin had his face not been wet with tears and frozen in fear rather than a blank expression.

"Got him, Dave," Bill said. He studied the man carefully. Just like the other five, he was sitting on the sidewalk, his back against the building, legs splayed out on front of him. "How long do I have?"

"Don't know," the radio voice crackled. "Maybe five. Not long enough."

"Gonna have to be. I'm going to get this one."

The first blast went off at the Hasty Shoppe Corner Market at eight. Witnesses described a man in an orange backpack sitting outside the place before the explosion. It wasn't uncommon in the area. Vagrants sat at the entrance to almost every shop and restaurant, begging for change or asking somebody to buy them a Coke. Nobody had thought much of a homeless man with a backpack sitting on the sidewalk. They went about their day, ignoring him or dropping the occasional bit of change at his feet. The man wasn't homeless. He wore neatly pressed Dockers and a button-down Oxford shirt. Security footage showed him walk up to the market, turn around toward the busy street and then sit down. Fifteen minutes later, the bomb exploded, killing him, four people passing by, and injuring ten people inside the store.

It happened four more times on the same street before anyone figured it out. They evacuated and cordoned off the streets, then sent in the sweepers. They didn't see him the first pass down the street, so Bill reckoned somebody was playing a mean gambit with these pawns. They had no information from the previous five. Bill was hoping for something with the sixth.

Problem was, he didn't know how long Number Six had been there. According to the pattern seen on the security cameras, they had fifteen minutes. Bill was certain that he had less than that.

"Anything?" Bill asked. He maintained a visual through the periscope.

"Camera went down about an hour ago. We got nothing."

Bill shook his head. This guy had information. He could tell them something. Not only that, he was still in one piece, and until he wasn't, they had time.

"I'm going out," Bill said.

"Negative," Dave barked. "You don't know how long on that timer, Bill."

"So, we're just going to watch him die? No." Bill grabbed the green padded suit. He opened the back door of the unit and climbed out. He donned it as fast as he could then settled the helmet on the high padded shoulders and started across the street. Bill was ten meters away when then man called out to him.

"No closer." Sweat and tears dripped from the man's face. In both hands, he held a round cylinder that was attached by wires to the backpack. An over-sized digital watch was clipped to the front strap.

"Easy man. I'm here to help," Bill said. He held up his hands and inched closer. "What's going on?"

The man shook his head. "Just go. You can't help."

Bill was only a meter away. The cheap plastic watch counted out time in stopwatch mode. It read 9:03. The cylinder was a pressure switch. There were two metal contact pads and the man's bare hands touched the metal. If he let go, it would trigger the explosives. Bill had six minutes to come up with a solution. "What's your name?"

The man looked at him blankly through his tears, then nodded as the question registered. "Mark."

"OK, Mark. Look, no bullshit, we don't have much time, but I'm getting you out of here."

"You can't," Mark said. "I can't let go. It will blow up if I do."

"Yeah, looks like it," Bill said. He looked at the watch.

10:34

"Did you want to do this Mark?" Bill asked. "This wasn't your idea, was it?"

Mark shook his head.

"No? Whoever did this is an asshole, and we're not going to let him win.

"He's going to win," Mark said as he sobbed.

Bill really didn't have time to argue the point. The watch said 11:45.

"Bill, get the fuck out of there. That's an order," Dave yelled in his ear.

"We can't lose this one," Bill said into his comm.

"No time. We'll find the next one."

"Bullshit. We've got this one," Bill said. He looked down at the backpack and the trigger. The man was shaking, and he had pissed his pants. The watch read 13:23. "Dave, I'm going to send this guy out.

"Damn it Billy—"

Bill shut off his comm. He took off his gloves. The watch read 13:45.

"One motion, move it up and I'll slide mine on. Then pull your arm out of the pack." Bill placed his right hand on the cylinder below Mark's. "On three, I'll count. One, two, three."

It worked.

13:57

He had Mark remove his arm from the strap.

"Same drill, left hand," Bill grabbed the trigger. "Go."

14:23

Bill held the trigger in both hands and Mark was free. "Run. Tell them everything. I got this." Mark hesitated, but Bill shook his head. "Go."

Mark took off. The watch said 14:51.

For the last nine seconds, Bill felt calm. He was at peace. When he let go of the trigger, he smiled.

LUCKY #48

"Oh my word!"

Muriel clasped her chest, her face aching from the stretch of her sudden, surprised smile. The announcement choked from tinny speakers, reverberating off the booths and masses of people.

"Again, the winner is lucky number 48! C'mon down to the stage and claim your prize!"

Muriel lifted her tray again. The number 48 was there, all right, crudely scripted in red marker. Others around her in the food court were eating and mumbling to each other, indifferent to her luck.

Bloody fools, she thought, clucking her dry tongue. "These swine wouldn't know class and winning if it struck them square in their inbred noses."

She set her tray down and shifted the plate of

chicken fingers to the table, next to her boat of ranch. A few grunts and heaves later, she was out of her chair and comfortably seated on her Rascal, tray in hand.

"Stanley! Isn't this grand?"

Stanley continued eating his turkey leg, taking no notice of her glee.

"Ingrate," she snarled, adjusting her pearl necklace. "I'm tickled a fine shade of pink, thank you very much."

The Rascal whirred down the aisle toward the back of the arena where the announcer sat perched on the stage. Muriel passed booths with vendors pedaling long-lasting lip stain, homemade candles smelling of soft baked goods, and silver jewelry that caught the gleam of the spastic fluorescent lighting with glittering fervor. Muriel turned her nose up at the cheap baubles and trinkets, keeping one hand on her winning tray lest someone snatch her deserved prize.

Muriel beamed with callous pride, flashing the bottom of the winning tray at vendors as she passed. She teased her silver, perfectly permed hair with the tips of her manicured fingers.

No one smiled. No one acknowledged her win or her glee.

"Sour bunch, the lot of you," Muriel mumbled under her breath.

The air became warm and stagnant. Muriel swiped

a hand across her forehead, beads of sweat smearing across her sagging skin.

"I'm positivity melting."

She looked at the vendors. They weren't smiling. They were scowling. Angry. Hateful. Some bared their teeth as she passed, others cussed at her in venomous whispers.

"Well I *never*!"

Muriel pushed on the throttle, willing the Rascal to go faster than it could. She was sweating profusely now, the armpits and thighs of her emerald velour track suit soaked with sweat. The smell of scented candles was far behind her, replaced by a bouquet of burnt hair and rotting meat. She gagged, her gorge bubbling acid and panic.

"What in the world—"

Now the vendors were smiling. Amused. Teeth sharp and elongated, blood dripping from cracked lips, mouths stretched and torn from ear to ear. Muriel's heart beat a forceful staccato against her rib cage, her pulse cymbals smashing inside her head.

The Rascal would go no faster. She abandoned it, grunts leaking out of her as she bore her own weight. The beasts mocked her, grunting and groaning, mimicking her strain.

"Sweet baby Jesus," she mewled as she hurried

away, pushing towards the stage as fast as her jiggling legs would carry her.

The vendors screamed, cawing like rabid banshees. They were hideous beasts with exposed ribcages and contorted spines, talons, and long, black tongues inserted in orifices both high and low. A salesman at a booth selling pots and pans was elbow deep in his own abdomen, ripping out his intestines and coiling them on the table. He saw her and giggled, bubbles of blood-tinged spittle dribbling off his cankered lips.

Muriel knew she was screaming. She could feel her stomach muscles straining and hot air moving across her tongue. Her voice, however, was drowned out by braying and profanity, violence and exuberant bloody coitus escalating all around her. Even the other attendees were tainted, rolling around on the floor at her feet, bones shattered and exposed, grabbing ahold of each other and eating the flesh off each others bones.

A young couple, no eyes in their sockets and flesh marred by deep talon gouges, were fornicating on the ground across the aisle. Muriel was too focused on the surrounding horror to notice the gore beneath. She tripped on the girl's legs and came crashing to the floor in a puddle of blood and human meat. She flailed, smearing blood angels on the concrete floor as ghouls and demons ripped and shredded her clothing until she was exposed and vulnerable.

She looked up for help, for understanding, for anything.

She found him, perched upon the stage, on a rotting throne made of bones and teeth bound together with strips of flesh and braids of hair.

"Welcome, lucky number 48! You are quite the lucky lady today!"

He was large, at least three meters tall, with rippling muscles on every inch of his gleaming crimson body. The horns on his head were coiled, tips gored into the sides of his head and exiting through his eyes. His tongue licked out like a serpent, black and thick and meaty, toying with the obsidian shaft between his legs.

"Congratulations on your win, Muriel," he said, in a chorus of tones, guttural words from the pit of his stomach.

Muriel wanted to run, to scream for help, to leave that trade show, never to return again. She was better than this. Than all of this.

She looked behind, way behind, to the place she had started her journey. Through a sea of writhing and gyrating monsters and a bath of blood and pain, she saw Stanley, screaming and sobbing.

And herself, splayed out on the floor, eyes wide and still. The trade show paramedics were pumping away on her chest and blasting breath into her mouth, but it was too late.

Muriel looked at the tray in her hands. That lucky number 48 stared back at her, a wolf in sheep's clothing.

Laughing.

SHOW OF POWER

FADE IN:

EXT. STREETS OF PARIS 1971-DAY

A parade is marching down the Champs-Elysees in Paris. We hear a military band playing La Marseillaise, the French national anthem. We see L'Arc de Triumphe in the distance. The sides of the street are crowded with people watching the parade.

.   .   .

LILIANE and **CLAUDE** are weaving through the crowd against the direction of the parade. Claude is pulling her, his hand grasping her bicep. Liliane is wearing a wide-bottom pant suit and a yellow cloche hat. She has a visible black eye.

LILIANE

(whispering)
Claude, stop, you're hurting me.

CLAUDE

Stop dawdling, then.

Claude yanks Liliane's arm, jerking her up beside him. She runs into a **WOMAN**.

LILIANE

Oh goodness, I'm sorry.

The woman looks at Liliane's face.

.   .   .

WOMAN

Oh love, are you...

Liliane keeps walking and tries to hide her face with her cloche.

LILIANE

The entire parade will march past if we stay still.

CLAUDE

I don't care about this stupid fucking music.

Liliane's lower lip quivers.

LILIANE

I love the bands.

CLAUDE

You're always missing the point. Military parades are about showing power. Flexing muscle.

. . .

Claude continues to pull Liliane through the crowd until they reach an open spot at the side of the road.

LILIANE

How about here?

Claude steps in front of Liliane so they are nose to nose. He squeezes her arms, and she winces at the pain.

CLAUDE

Why are you tormenting me? I said I didn't want to watch the stupid fucking bands.

Claude points at the street where a line of trumpet players are passing by.

CLAUDE (CONT'D)

Are you too stupid to see that's a band?

.   .   .

Liliane's chest heaves as she draws in a deep breath.

LILIANE

Yes I know, but the bands will pass soon. And this is a front row spot. You'll be able to see the troops and vehicles quite clearly from here.

Claude narrows his eyes but releases his grip.

CLAUDE

I'm going to get food. Stay.

Claude walks away.

Standing next to Liliane is **MONIQUE**, a beautiful woman with short dark hair. She is wearing high-waisted shorts, a sleeveless shirt, and a black beret. Monique is smiling and clapping along with the music.

Monique looks at Liliane and her smile fades.

.   .   .

Liliane offers an awkward smile, then hunches her shoulders and hides her face with her hand.

MONIQUE

Aren't they wonderful?

LILIANE

Pardon?

MONIQUE

The bands. They're my favorite part of the parade.

Liliane relaxes her shoulders and smiles.

LILIANE

Mine too.

Suddenly, Liliane stops smiling and looks over her shoulder.

. . .

MONIQUE

Are you okay?

LILIANE

I'm...

Liliane wrings her hands and looks at the ground.

MONIQUE

(after watching Liliane for a moment)
I'm Monique.

Monique reaches her hand out to Liliane, and Liliane
flinches. Monique pulls her hand back.

LILIANE

Sorry. I'm Liliane.

MONIQUE

Pleased to meet you, Liliane.

. . .

Liliane forces a smile then turns back to the parade. The passing band is playing Quand Madelon, a military march. Lilian closes her eyes and taps her foot along with the music.

LILIANE

My papa loved this song. When I was little, he would play it for me on his trumpet. He taught it to me on the clarinet.

MONIQUE

Sounds like your papa was a wonderful man.

Liliane nods and opens her eyes. Heavy tears spill down her cheeks. She wipes them away with the back of her hand.

The last marching band passes, Liliane's song fading as they move away. Now we hear feet marching on the pavement.

.   .   .

Rows of military personnel pass by, dressed in uniform.

Lilian's mouth falls open in shock.

MONIQUE
What's wrong?

Lilian points to **FEMALE PERSONNEL #1**, a woman with long hair tied in a knot at the base of her neck, her curvaceous body filling out her uniform.

LILLIAN
A... woman?

MONIQUE
(scoffing, surprised)
Have you been living under a rock?

Liliane shrugs and hooks her thumb toward Claude.

. . .

Monique pulls a newspaper from her Macrame handbag and passes it to Liliane, pointing at the front page news.

The newspaper, dated July 14th, 1971, reads, "Today marks the first time in history female personnel will march in the Bastille Day Military Parade."

MONIQUE

Isn't it wonderful? About time.

Liliane looks up at the cadets. She pokes the air, counting the women in the parade.

LILIANE

So many...

Liliane touches the bruise on her face.

LILIANE

Papa wanted that for me, you know. To be strong.

.   .   .

Claude returns, stepping between Liliane and Monique.

CLAUDE
(under his breath)
Whore.

MONIQUE
Excuse me?

Claude turns his back to Monique.

CLAUDE
Liliane, at least you know better than to show all that skin.

Claude hands Liliane a foil-wrapped potato.

CLAUDE
I got you a baked potato. God knows it'll still go

straight to your thighs, but there wasn't much for healthy choices.

Liliane looks down at the potato, staring at it while Claude bites into a juicy burger, chewing loudly.

Liliane looks up at the rows of marching personnel. She makes eye contact with FEMALE PERSONNEL #2.

FEMALE PERSONNEL #2 smiles and nods at Liliane.

Liliane smashes the potato into Claude's chest.

CLAUDE
What the bloody hell?

Claude clenches his fists and takes a step toward Liliane.

. . .

A nearby **POLICE OFFICER** walks toward them, stepping between Claude and Liliane.

POLICE OFFICER

Is there a problem here, Mademoiselle?

LILIANE

Goodbye, Claude.

Liliane walks by Monique and looks at her.

LILIANE

Wanna catch up to the bands and listen to some music?

Monique laughs and flips Claude the bird.

Liliane and Monique lace their fingers together and hurry away, skipping alongside the parade toward the marching bands.

.   .   .

FADE OUT.

CHECKPOINT FIVE

FADE IN:
    INT. SURVEILLANCE VAN

DAVE EDGAR reclines in his chair. He is visibly tired with dark circles under his eyes. His clothing, a uniform with a name patch that says **EDGAR** is wrinkled and disheveled.

The van is littered with trash. It has several video feeds, audio surveillance panels and equipment, and a digital map of the area.

Edgar's feet are propped up on the instrument panel of the van. His eyes are closed, and he yawns.

When an **OPERATOR VOICE (OS)** comes

through over his comm, he jolts awake, nearly falling out of the chair.

VOICE (OS)

Yo, Edgar, you awake?

Edgar rubs his eyes, adjusts his headset, and shakes himself awake before answering.

EDGAR

Of course I am.

VOICE (LAUGHING)

Liar

EDGAR

Piss off, Chambers.

CHAMBER'S (OS)

Relief should be coming in five. He checked in here. I'm sending him your way.

.   .   .

EDGAR

About fucking time.

CHAMBER'S (OS)

Don't act like you got it so rough Edgar. Some would be happy to be in your position, whacking off in that van while we freeze our asses off.

Edgar looks annoyed by the comment but shakes his head in the affirmative as if he's heard it before. He rolls his eyes and nods, then flips off the comm system.

EDGAR

I don't make the assignments.

Edgar looks at the digital map. There are dots on the map that form a ring all the way around the area. The dots are all concentrated at five checkpoints. There are three dots per checkpoint.

Edgar also has a camera feed at each of the checkpoints that shows him a defense point with a large caliber gun and breastworks. He looks at a Checkpoint, number one, and he sees a soldier walk out.

EDGAR

He's the relief?

CHAMBERS

Affirmative. Baby-faced and ready to fall in love.

EDGAR

I got his signal. Send him.

The digital map cuts out for a second, as do all the video feeds. They come back in a second or two, but Edgar has a panicked look.

EDGAR (FRIGHTENED AND CONFUSED)

All Checkpoints, report in. I lost all of you for a second.

What the hell was that?

CHAMBERS (AFTER A BRIEF PAUSE)

Nothing here. You're like a chicken shit old lady Edgar.

· · ·

Edgar rolls his eyes again but scans all the video feeds. They're all broadcasting normally.

EDGAR

Something happened. Add it to your logs. Chambers, send that fucking relief and tell him to double time it.

CHAMBERS (LAUGHING)

Roger that, Grandma.

Edgar hears other laughter over the comm. His face contorts with anger and annoyance as he fights the urge to respond. He stays quiet.

The extra blip starts to move away from Checkpoint One and toward him. It stops at his location on the map.

The camera feeds cut out again and the map is gone for a second. They all come back at the same time.

Edgar looks terrified. He bangs the side of the equipment as if that can help.

EDGAR
(NERVOUS AND SERIOUS)
Everybody report in.

There is only static on all the radio channels. Edgar jumps when he hears the knock at the back of the van.

There's a camera feed at the van door. Edgar checks it and notes the **BABY-FACED RELIEF** standing there. He looks scared as he holds up an ID card and scans the area around the van nervously.

Edgar presses a button. The van doors open and the baby-faced relief climbs in.

Edgar closes the doors quickly. Edgar regards the other man.

. . .

BABY-FACED RELIEF (NERVOUSLY)

Anders.

EDGAR

You see anything out there?

Anders shakes his head. His uniform is perfect. Starched, immaculate. Every thread and button in place.

ANDERS

Nothing.

Edgar checks all the feeds again.

EDGAR

All quiet. No movement.

Edgar checks the map.

EDGAR

I see everybody but… (he opens the comm and hails them all) hey, morons, knock it off and check in.

. . .

ANDERS

Is the communication system malfunctioning?

Edgar shoots Anders an annoyed look.

EDGAR

I'd say so, genius.

Edgar tries a few things, but the comm system remains static. He's panicked as he mashes buttons.

EDGAR

Nothing going on in this place for three months, now this? Right when I could leave? Fuck this.

ANDERS

Surely there is a logical explanation. You've seen no signs of activity?

Edgar shakes his head as he checks all the feeds again.

EDGAR

Not a thing. It's been boring as hell and they didn't tell us what we were looking for.

Anders begins to relax his body. He stands up and straightens his uniform so that it's perfect again.

Edgar looks at the map. He notices something strange at Checkpoint Three.

EDGAR

Something's wrong. Their signals are out.

Anders joins him at the map. He looks concerned, but not afraid, like Edgar.

ANDERS

Maybe it's just a glitch.

EDGAR (IN A SCOFFING TONE)

A glitch? And no comm? What unit did you come from? The stupid one?

Edgar's eyes widen.

. . .

EDGAR

There. Look. Four and Two are gone. All of them!

He points to the screen and there are no signal dots at Four or at Two. He points to Checkpoint One and to the van at Five. He points to Checkpoint One as the signal dots disappear.

EDGAR (DESPERATELY, INTO THE COMM)

Chambers! You asshole! Come on! Answer me!

Edgar is surprised to see a red splatter all over the map. It's chunky, and globs of fat and blood obscure the readout.

Edgar looks down and sees a black clawed hand protruding from his stomach. He stares, confused.

The claw pulls back through him and he screams as he's spun around and collapses against the instrument console.

.   .   .

Anders is standing over him, smiling. One of his hands is a normal human hand, the other a hideous black claw, slick with Edgar's blood.

Anders raises the bloody claw to his mouth and licks it clean, his face ecstatic and enraptured as he licks every drop of blood and glob of tissue from the claw.

Edgar screams as Anders' face contorts into a black demon's face. His head has gnarled horns and his mouth is full of jagged shark's teeth.

Anders opens his gaping maw and screams in Edgar's face.

Edgar screams as Anders attacks him.

Anders rips Edgar apart and eats him.

EXT. VAN-DAY

Anders exits the van. He is in full demon form. His

uniform is covered in blood and his face is smeared with red.

Anders exhales and smiles, all his bloody teeth showing, then looks up and shivers. He vibrates reverts to human form.

Anders smiles. He straightens his uniform and begins to whistle a happy tune as he walks away from the van.

FADE OUT

HE'S MINE

The chicken clucked and squawked. The sound of the bird echoed off the rocks, audible over the crash of the waves as they broke on the rocky shore. She shifted the chicken's weight to get a better hold on it, but she didn't try to discourage the animal's noise. After a few moments of waiting and nothing happening, she pinched the bird again, hard. It pecked her hand and screeched. She almost dropped the wretched thing, but she managed a hold on one of its legs. They tussled a bit, but she finally secured the creature.

The sun was gone now, only a tiny slice of its red-orange glow visible on the far horizon of the sea. The water was dark, inky black, and it crashed hard as the tide rolled in, higher and higher up the rocky shore.

This was the dangerous time. You could be swept out to sea in the powerful undertow or you might encounter the predators that fed at this hour, sharks, and other things that used the diminishing light to their advantage. The old women told tales of creatures that haunted the dark water. In hushed whispers around warm, bright kitchen fires, they told stories. They blushed and giggled like schoolgirls as they told them, but always underlying the innuendo was a fear. She always listened carefully to the stories, but when she asked questions, the old women shushed her and told her she had no business listening. They shooed her from the kitchen, but she heard enough.

She brought the offering, and she waited patiently, but nothing happened. The waves seemed to calm a bit. She was ready to give up, creep back to her father's house when she saw them. Yellow eyes gleamed on the surface of the water. She spotted four pairs. A barking noise came from the water, and she could hear differences in the sounds, like the differences in human voices, which suggested to her they were talking to one another. Finally, one deep sounding bark was the loudest. The rest quieted and their eyes disappeared below the water.

She strained her eyes to see in the moonlight, to make out a shape, but all she could see was a gigantic dark blob coming in from the wave line. It heaved itself upon the sand then limped and slithered to her. She stood still—afraid and curious at the same time—as it approached. The creature stopped a few feet from her and cocked its head, then barked and snarled. It was hideous. It looked like one of the seals that littered the shoreline, but different. Larger, with sleek black fur, and while seals had flippers, this creature had elongated hands, webbed, but distinctly human with long pink fingers. Its face was dog-like, with a short muzzle and those yellow eyes. When it opened its mouth and barked at her, she saw rows and rows of jagged teeth, like a shark's, and she smelled its foul, rotten fish breath.

It barked and growled again, then looked at the chicken in her arms. She looked down at the bird, then held it out toward the creature. It reached out slowly with those pink webbed fingers and gently took the chicken from her. It sniffed the animal and hesitated a moment, then growled and shoved the chicken into its jagged maw, ripping and tearing through feathers and flesh until blood stained both its face and the sand below.

When it finished, it came for her. She didn't move. The old women were all united about that. Move or show fear and you die. It sniffed her: her hair, her face, her body as it circled her, growling softly in her ear as it did. She felt the fear course through her, but she felt something else also. Thrilling. The creature knew it too, could probably smell both, she reasoned. She felt flushed and her heart thundered in her chest as she stood still.

It stopped and looked her in the eyes with those yellow eyes that looked human. That unnatural shade of yellow bored into her. It cocked its head again and made a noise, not a bark, but a guttural, low noise and somehow, she knew it was a question and, unbelievably, she knew how to answer. "To see you," she said.

It nodded and smiled wide, showing the rows of teeth, then it heaved its bulk upright, balancing on its back flippers. It was huge, towering over her at well over six feet tall. It reached up with the long pink fingers and dug its nails into its own flesh. It screamed as it ripped and tore at itself, folding back the fur and flesh. As it did, a form began to emerge from the folds of bloody fur. First a head, then an arm and shoulder cleared the blubbery bulk. It extracted its other arm and screamed again, then pushed the bloody folds of fur down the length of its body. It stepped free from the flesh and she stared.

He was covered in blood and small bits of yellow fat, but she paid little mind to that because to her, he was the most beautiful man she had ever seen. Tall, broad-shouldered, and perfectly muscled, his hair looked fair as the moonlight glittered off it. He held out his hand to her and said something in his language as he nodded to the water. She hesitated, because of her long dress, but he smiled at her and asked again, and she nodded. She took off the garment but kept her sheer muslin shift and held her arms across her chest self-consciously. He wasn't modest in any way, naked as he was, and he laughed at her as he uncrossed her arms. He looked at her body for a moment and smiled. He said something in his language, his voice deep and low. She didn't need to understand the words to comprehend what he said and she felt her face flush. He took her hand and led her out into the water. He stopped when he was waist deep, nearly chest deep to her, and he washed the blood from his body. She reached out and touched his chest, tracing the muscles along it and down his sides. He made a happy noise at that and stepped closer. He took her hand and dipped it in the water, then used it to wash his chest. After a few repeats, she took over and needed no further instruction.

When he was clean, he dipped down and disappeared below the water. She jumped when she felt hands on her legs, sliding up and under her shift, up her calves, her thighs. His hands stopped there, and his yellow eyes peeked out of the water. He said something to her, a question, and she nodded yes. He smiled and stood up, and in one motion, removed her shift over her head and tossed it into the water. He pulled her to him and kissed her. It was slow at first, then she got greedy. It wasn't like kissing Tommy McNamara, with the floppy, dry lips and stale beer breath. This was gentle but firm and she could taste both the sea salt and blood on his lips. She wanted more, and she pressed herself against him. He picked her up, and she wrapped her legs around his waist as he carried her out of the sea. He took her in the sand, so many times that she lost count and the concept of time seemed unnatural.

She was groggy and sore and sandy when he finally untangleddisentangled himself from her. She protested—grabbed him and held on—but he pointed to the thin line of light on the horizon and said something to her.

"You'll come back?" she asked.

He cupped her cheek, kissed her, then whispered something in her ear. She shivered as his lips touched her earlobe.

He shrugged back into his skin, screaming as he did. When he was complete again, he ambled back off into the surf. She found her shift down the shore, wet, sandy, and useless. She didn't bother with it. She pulled her dress back on and went home.

The next night a storm blew in and she couldn't go to the shore. She paced and fretted the whole night as she stared out the window at the sea. It stormed three more nights, but the weather blew itself out on the fourth day, and that night was cool, calm, and quiet. The sun was gone and the moon had risen, its silver light illuminating the entire beach as the waves lapped calmly at the shore. This time she had brought a lamb, only a few months old. Her father wouldn't miss it. The babies disappeared from time to time. The little thing was soft, and she stroked its coat as she waited, scanning the water obsessively. The lamb bleated, hungry and looking for its mother.

Finally, she saw the yellow eyes, five pairs of them. Her heart began to pound in her chest. She heard the familiar barking and snarling as they argued amongst themselves. He waddled out of the surf to her. He destroyed the lamb, but she never noticed the carnage. She could barely wait for him to finish and emerge from the skin. When he finally did, she didn't wait for him to rinse off, she threw herself on him and they tumbled into the surf. Once again, she begged him not to leave her, but he pulled himself away at dawn.

Every night she could get away, she did. The offerings varied. Her father started missing the farm animals, so she began taking strays and pets. People whispered in the village about pookas and hobs, and the old women at the hearth whispered about her. Her stomach grew round and her father cursed her and beat her. He whipped Tommy McNamara, who claimed to have had no part in her condition, which was true. The men in the village helped, but the old women, they knew better. They made signs over her when she walked by, and looked at her sadly.

When her father threw her out, nobody would help her, save one old crone who lived out on a cliff by herself. Everyone in the town whispered about her too, calling her a witch, and spitting at her when she came into town to buy things. She went to live with the old woman in the little house on the cliff and her belly grew heavy and oddly shaped. When the baby was born, the old woman took her time cleaning him and wrapping him. The crone held him close and waited before she let her see him.

"He's mine. Let me have him," she told the old woman.

"He's not yours," the old crone said. "He belongs to them. It's best you just let me give him back."

"He is mine!" She grabbed for the baby, but the old woman pulled him away.

"When you see him, you'll know," the old woman said as she handed the baby to her.

When she unwrapped the blanket, she screamed. His face was lumpy and misshapen with a partial muzzle and a fine smattering of silky brown fur all over it. His legs were tiny stumps, even for a baby, and the feet were long, like paddles. His little torso was also covered in patchy brown fur, but it was the hands that upset her the most. They were human, but elongated and webbed. He flailed them around as he cried.

She tried to nurse him, but he wouldn't eat. Her milk was barely coming, anyway. The old woman tried to tell her again that she should give him back to the sea, that he would never nurse and would die anyway, but she kept trying. Finally, she gave up after he cried for a week straight and she hadn't slept. "What do I do?" she asked the old woman.

"Throw him over the cliff and into the sea," the old woman said.

"No! He'll die. I won't murder him." She hugged the screaming baby close. "I-I'll take him to them."

"That you cannot do," the old woman said, shaking her head.

"I can, and I will," she said. "He'll come. He'll come for us. I know he will. He loves me."

"Do as you please then," the old woman said. She looked at her with a sad, knowing finality.

She waited until nightfall, then she took the baby down to the shore. The baby cried loudly. He was hungry and cold. She held him close to her chest and tried not be repulsed at the feel of his oily, patchy fur against her skin. Her heart fluttered in her chest and she smiled when at last she saw the yellow eyes appear in the surf.

He waddled on shore, barking angrily to the others. They followed him ashore. He tore his skin off and the others did the same. She had never seen any of the others before and she marveled at their beauty. The females were beauties with round, firm breasts, perfectly made faces, and long, curly hair of every shade. The males were all beautiful too, muscular and perfect. None were quite as beautiful to her as he was, though, and her heart stuttered when he finally approached her. He didn't smile or kiss her, he only looked at the poor, starving creature in her arms. He motioned to the baby and whispered something in his language that sounded sad. She held the tiny wailing thing out to him, and for the first time since he was born, the baby stopped crying. He cooed to him and spoke to him, and soon the baby was asleep. He kissed its forehead then turned and handed the sleeping mite to a woman. She sang softly to him and all the women crowded around her and joined in. The men put on their meat suits and splashed back into the sea. The women followed and took the little creature with them.

She was happy, and she tried to embrace him. She wanted nothing more than to go with him, to be with him forever, but he held her at arm's length and he looked sad.

"I'll come with you," she said, motioning to the sea. "I want to be with you."

He shook his head and let her go. She begged and pleaded with him, but he refused to listen or to even kiss her goodbye. He shoved himself into his fur and blubber and started back to the black water. She screamed as he waded back into the sea and disappeared.

She sat on the shore and cried, adding salt to the sea and cursing the waves. When she was almost all cried out, she saw the yellow eyes appear in the surf again and she smiled. He had come back for her.

She pushed herself off the sand and discarded her clothes, throwing them behind her as she waded into the sea to be with him. The eyes moved farther away with each of her steps, leading her out into the deep until she couldn't touch and she had to tread water.

The eyes were still there. She heard his distinct, familiar bark. More yellow eyes appeared around her, dozens of them, and dozens of barks answered him, then suddenly, they all disappeared below. She turned in a circle, looking all around her, but she saw nothing but black, glassy water in every direction. She felt something bump her toe, then something brushed past her thigh. She smiled, thinking he was playing with her, but her smiled faded when something crashed into her more forcefully, pushing her through the water. She screamed when something bit into her leg and released her, then again, but this time her scream ended in a gurgle as it bit into her ankle and pulled her down into the water. She choked and flailed as he ripped her apart. Somewhere in the distance, through the water, she heard a baby cry.

PLEASE

The air tasted like muddy shoes. The sun was setting, an orange kiss on the horizon, and Agatha knew she had to hurry or her father would worry. And worry would turn to anger, and anger to pain.

Plus, she was hungry.

On long, slender legs she scurried through the lich-gate, ducking around tombstones and bunches of tear-soaked flowers until she saw him, a silhouette against the pink sky. Tall and dark, the groundskeeper was bent over a fresh grave, toiling, his skeletal limbs tilling the fresh dirt, upsetting the stench of rot and death.

Agatha approached him from behind, noting the twitch of his muscles, the protrusion of his knobby, crooked spine through his stained white t-shirt as he heaved and pulled through the dirt, smoothing the fresh mound. Even his sounds were feral, the wet grunts of a trifling pig, and sweaty drool hung from his lower lip like a spider's thread.

"Mister?"

His rake made a thud as it fell from his hands and hit the dirt. Jaw agape, he gawked at her, straining his beady, black eyes to see her beneath the thick dusk.

"What you want, chil'?"

Agatha twirled a lock of her curly red hair through her pale fingers.

"Please?"

Holding her breath deep in her belly, Agatha waited while the groundskeeper considered her, searching her body, licking his lips.

"No," he said, a grumble beneath his breath. "Go 'way."

His elongated arm dragged across the dirt and scooped up his rake. His toil continued, his back to her once more, the conversation killed for the time being.

"Hrphm."

Arms crossed in a quiet tantrum, she spun on purple converse runners and stomped away, leaving the groundskeeper and his dead behind.

The room was filled with the sounds of bums shuffling in seats, the murmurs of whispers, and the click and scratch of Mrs. Tyler's chalk across the board at the front of the room.

"Okay everyone," Mrs. Tyler said in her sing-song tones. "Today we are talking about The Outsiders."

The blank book report on Agatha's desk mocked her, taunting her with the duties of seventh grade rather than letting her figure out what she was going to do about that pesky groundskeeper. If the rumors about him were true, the playground chatter, the whispers in the dark… he was the only one who could help her now. But what could a ghoul like him possibly want? A bowl of rats for breakfast?

Agatha snickered, drawing Mrs. Tyler's attention.

"Something funny, Agatha?"

Twenty-two faces turned toward Agatha, and, like a rush from the furnace, her face grew hot with embarrassment.

"No, ma'am."

"Seems to me you've been daydreaming a lot lately." Mrs. Tyler's mouth was open, as if she intended to continue, but she did not. Her lips pressed together softly, and her eyes moistened as she regarded Agatha.

"See me after class, please." Her tone was not angry, like Agatha was about to be given extra work. Her voice was coated in sadness. Pity.

Agatha did not want pity. She was already bursting at the seams from everyone's pity and concern and thoughts and prayers. They didn't do jack shit.

But she would toe the line, see Mrs. Tyler after class, hear about how sorry she was and if there was anything she could do to help. Agatha would assure her that it was hard, but she was managing, and she would do a better job paying attention in class. They would hug, and Mrs. Tyler would go about her merry way while Agatha stayed firmly cemented in place, caught in her despair.

But not for long.

Tammy Walker's glittering iPhone case caught Agatha's eye from across the room. Tammy was the only girl in the whole of seventh grade to have a phone, and it was the new iPhone. Everyone ooh'd and awed over it in the cafeteria, even though Tammy could only use it to play baby games and call her mommy when she needed rides and new toys. Tammy always had the latest and greatest, and never appreciated it. Not one little bit.

Agatha loathed Tammy, but that was a lovely iPhone…

"Please?"

Agatha thrust the glittering pink phone toward the groundskeeper who stood in the doorway of his wither old shed, eyeballing the trinket.

"Where you get tha'?"

"I stoled it. While Terrible Tammy wasn't looking. She puts it in the side drink pocket of her knapsack, so it was super easy to snag it while she walked down the hall flirtin' with all the boys."

The groundskeeper's brow furrowed into an angry caterpillar as he evaluated the offering. Like a set of talons, his boney fingers unfurled, reaching for the phone and scraping it from the palm of Agatha's hand. She shuddered at the feel of his leathery old-man flesh, cold and waxy. Smelled bad, too, like when her dog threw up.

"Huh," he said. "It's a might' good try, but nah."

With a flick and crack of his wrist, he tossed the phone out into the cemetery and slammed the door in her face. The sound of the phone bouncing off a head-stone shot straight through Agatha's bones, drawing tears to her eyes. She didn't even look at the shattered screen as she walked away, leaving the glittering pink treasure in the dirt of the dead.

Dinner smelled delicious, but Agatha had no appetite.

She finished up at the cemetery earlier than the day before—the sun was not yet touching the horizon this time—and would actually be able to sit with her father in time for dinner. That meant no scolding and a hot meal.

Her father chewed slowly, his eyes dark and distance, the table silent as they forced down their burgers and fries. Four nights that week they had ordered takeaway; the other three were mac and cheese or a bowl of cereal. Agatha didn't mind. She didn't much care for food anymore. Her black lab Dante rested her head in Agatha's lap, and Agatha stroked her dark fur rather than giving any attention to the food on her plate.

The empty place setting was a beacon in the dim and dirty dining room, a constant reminder of the vacancy in their little family. Every so often, Agatha's eyes would flicker to the gold trim on her mama's favorite plate, the last piece of china she'd ever eaten from. Now it was moldy, littered with remnants of mashed potatoes and shriveled green beans.

"What you lookin' at, girl?"

Eyes back down on her own plate, Agatha crossed her hands in her lap.

"Nothin' daddy."

"Ain't look like nothin."

She didn't raise her eyes, but she knew her daddy

was looking at that plate, too. When she looked up at his face, it was scrunched with the sadness.

"Did it to her own goddamn self, you know." His words were slurred, punctuated by a calloused finger tapping the edge of his glass of bourbon.

Agatha knew. She would never forget the red shimmer of the bath water, the way it soaked up into her mama's curls, staining them such a pretty crimson. That image haunted her, the nothingness in her mama's eyes as she lay there, sprawled in the bath, arm sliced open and hanging over the edge…

"Eat, girl. Quit mopin'."

The tension in the room shattered as Agatha slammed her fork down on her plate. Dante yelped as Agatha pushed away from the table and ran for the door, trying to escape the room before her daddy could see the tears flow.

"Girl?"

His words weren't kind or loving—he didn't have that in him—but they were more gentle than she expected. She turned to him. He struggled, his lips seeming to search for words they couldn't find, until he looked up at her and nodded.

"It's gonna be okay. We're gonna be okay."

"Yeah, Daddy. I know."

The sound of Tammy Walker's shrill laugh pierced straight into Agatha's brain, scraping like nails on a chalkboard, nearly making her heave. They were pointing and laughing, Tammy and her herd, at poor Simon Worchowski who had fallen on the running track, tangled in his untied laces for the umpteenth time that year. He was a tool, but he was harmless, and would grow out of his awkwardness.

"Leave him alone," Agatha said, kneeling to Simon's side and helping him to his feet.

"You guys BFF's now?" one girl said, hands on her hips. "He your boyfriend?"

"Naw," Tammy said, eyeing both Agatha and Simon from head to toe. "Ain't his style, that one. He don't like the ladies. Though this one looks like a boy, so maybe he interested."

Gales of laughter erupted from the gaggle of bullies. Simon winced, and Agatha reached out and grabbed his hand while the mean girls walked away. The smug expression on Tammy's face curdled Agatha's blood.

"Don't mind them," Agatha scoffed as she brushed the dirt off Simon's shirt.

But he did mind, she could tell. His lower lip quivered, and he looked haunted, like that poor boy who had been outed by his soccer team, and celebrated by making his last meal the barrel of his father's shotgun.

Simon walked away, but his despair lingered as rage roiled hot in Agatha's belly. But that rage sparked an idea, and that idea grew into a plan.

Agatha ran after Tammy, a newfound energy in her step.

"I don't get why you didn't say nothin' sooner," Tammy said, lips pursed.

"Honestly, I forgot," Agatha said.

The leaves in the ditch crunched as the girls strolled toward Agatha's trailer, a chorus of the death of summer.

"Why you didn't just bring it with you to school?" Tammy whined.

"Like I said. Forgot."

"Damn fool," Tammy said under her breath.

But Agatha heard, and it made the whole thing even easier.

Her daddy wasn't home when they got to the trailer. Agatha smiled. When they walked inside, the screen door was left unlatched, and the wind blew it against the siding in a repetitive staccato.

"Hand it over so I can get outta this dump," Tammy said, cringing at Agatha's living arrangements. Tammy's eyes drifted to the table, stopping at the dinner plate.

Bang, Bang, Bang.

Agatha's heart pounded every time the screen door struck the trailer.

The axe should have felt heavy in Agatha's grasp, like it always had when she chopped wood for Daddy. But now it was light as a feather.

"Don't look at that plate," Agatha growled through gritted teeth. "That belongs to Mama."

The cemetery was shrouded in full dark by the time Agatha arrived. She imagined her Daddy pacing on the gravel lane, ready to give her a whippin' as soon as she showed her face. But she wasn't worried. If things went right, her face wasn't gonna make an appearance there ever again.

The groundskeeper was leaned up against a tree, gnawing on a long, slender bone.

"What you want now, chil'?"

Agatha walked up to the man, looked up into his dark, cavernous eyes, and, with her slender fingers laced through the long, straight blonde hair, lifted Tammy's head to his face. Tammy's lower jaw had been removed, and her neck was dripping slow, thick blood, strips of skin dangling and swinging in the breeze.

Agatha drew a deep breath, releasing it in a hopeful word.

"Please."

The groundskeeper rolled the bone around his mouth, his eyes groping the severed head. His expression morphed from confused to surprised, finally settling on wicked glee; a smile stretched across his face, tearing his skin from ear to ear, black blood spilling down his white shirt and dirty khaki's. He laced his fingers though Tammy's hair and lifted the head from Agatha's grasp, bringing to his lips and suckling the blood from beneath her protruding tongue.

He laughed, and the ground shook. Agatha grasped her arms, the chill and terror causing her to shake. Once the end of his laughter choked out of him like a sputtering engine, he clutched the head to his chest and bent down to Agatha.

"Please?" she pleaded, fat tears streaming down her face.

"Okay."

He licked his tongue out—a vile, silver, forked mass of meat covered in blood—and licked the side of Agatha's face.

As he walked away, his hooves made tiny crunches

in the manicured lawn of the cemetery, until he had retreated inside his shed and shut the door.

Agatha stood there, coated in blood, shivering in the cold.

And she waited.

When she could not wait any longer, she yelled at the groundskeeper's shed.

"Well? What happens now?"

Angry, she ran over and pounded her fists against the rotting wood. The shed disintegrated into ash, and it contents crumbled to glowing embers. She stared at it, at the impossibility, then looked down the path towards the lichgate. The graves were moving, ever-so-slightly, heaving and moaning.

"Oh."

Agatha smiled.

She walked down the path, out of the lichgate, and in the ditch toward the trailer park. She passed the old rusted out mustang that had been on the side of the road since before her mama had died. The car was rocking, the windows steamy and wet. Agatha peered in the smashed-out windshield, and saw two creatures, black and scaled, one penetrating the other, gyrating and howling in pain and pleasure.

And on she went, past the old Thompson's corn-fields where beasts of fur and feather, talon and scale, fornicated and bit and ripped at each other, sending spurting fountains of black blood into the sky, peppering the night with a smattering of bloody stars.

By the time Agatha reached her trailer, sweat coated her body, trapped beneath her prepubescent breasts and soaking her armpits. Dante was sitting outside, guarding the door. But it wasn't Dante anymore, but a hideous beast with three heads—the two newest having sported from Dante's shoulders in a bloody explosion of tissue and bone and gore.

With each step up her driveway Agatha stripped off a piece of clothing until her toes touched the wooden steps leading to the side door. The flames flickering in a circle around the trailer danced off her naked, wet body—a slick, oily display—and the moisture evaporated into steam as she entered her home.

The table was set as it always was—two paper plates and Mama's fine china at the head of the table. Mama was perched on her chair like a throne, a crown of bones and bowels balanced on her massive, horned head, her crimson body rippling and twitching with muscle. Curling the obsidian talons she had for fingers, she beckoned Agatha. Agatha crawled into her mama's lap and cuddled into her heaving breasts.

"Welcome home," Mama said in a bitonal growl.

THE SHADE OF NIGHT

*S*omething's wrong.

Donna rolled the quiche around her mouth, trying to savor the explosion of flavors, the fluffiness of the egg.

But she couldn't.

"What's wrong, honey?"

Honey.

Until the last few days, Brock had been cold. Cruel, even. They'd only been married a few months, but Donna was surprised they had lasted this long. He had changed so drastically after the wedding.

"Shall we go?" she said. "I don't want to be late."

His eyes searched her face, a certain darkness in his expression.

"Of course."

They got their food to go. Donna hadn't had much of an appetite, but quiche was her favorite. Perhaps later she'd feel like nibbling it again.

A short jaunt upstairs and they were at the ophthalmologist. Besides having her favorite quiche, Brock had chosen the restaurant because it was right below the office.

"You didn't need to come," she said.

He's never come to any appointment before.

Maybe he felt guilty. He was the one who'd broken her glasses, after all.

"I just love spending time with you," he said, giving her hand a squeeze.

Bullshit.

The wait was excruciating. Brock flicked through a magazine with one hand while holding tight to her with the other. Though it was ridiculous, she felt restrained. Donna rested her hand on her roiling stomach, her fingers trembling with anxiety.

"Donna?" The receptionist's voice cut the air like a blade. "We're ready for you."

Brock, refusing to relinquish his grasp, yanked Donna's arm when she jumped out of her seat.

"You don't need to come in," Donna said. "It's just an eye appointment."

"It's okay," he said, smiling sweetly.

No really. Please don't.

Like a lost puppy, Donna followed the receptionist down the hall, legs weak, anxiety bubbling like toxic sludge in her throat. She should have just gone to the mall, to her regular ophthalmologist, but Brock took it upon himself to make her an appointment with this one.

He has to be in control of everything.

No matter. Her glasses were broken—another one of Brock's expressions of love—and she needed a new prescription.

The exam room was beautiful, rich red leather furniture and darkened walls, an assortment of gleaming optical equipment and apothecary items lining the oak counter. It had a dark charm, but Donna could appreciate none of it. A deepening sense of dread sunk its claws into her lungs, stealing her breath.

"Brock!"

The ophthalmologist was young, around Brock's age. They obviously knew each other, based on the exuberant greeting and firm pats on the back. They chatted for a moment, something about football or the stock market, Donna wasn't sure. She couldn't quite hear. Panic was ringing gongs in her ears.

"Just a regular exam today, yes?" The doctor seemed to take no notice of Donna's swelling anxiety.

That's good, Donna thought, ever the appeaser.

"Yes, thanks," she said, the words sputtering out. "New prescription."

"You're in the right place. It's what we do." Both the doctor and Brock broke out into gales of laughter, a noise that sent nuclear chills up Donna's spine.

Though the lights were already dim, the doctor dropped them further, the only lights a small spotlight on the eye chart and a headlamp on the doctor's head. It was disorienting, shadows dancing in the nooks of the tiny office, the white moon of her husband's face hovering in the corner like a spectre.

"Thanks so much, man, for fitting me in," Brock said.

Me? But it's my appointment…

"Not a problem," the doctor said. "It's been long enough."

Long enough?

That laughter again, throaty, booming. Saliva pooled under Donna's tongue, threatening to pour out on the floor.

"I… I don't feel so good."

The room was spinning, pirouetting just out of sync with her stomach. Sweat soaked her shirt and poured down into her eyes. Panic had grown into a behemoth, threatening to consume her whole. No stranger to chronic anxiety, Donna knew what she needed.

I need to get out of here.

"I can't… may I use the restroom?"

"Few more moments," the doctor said.

Brock handed a sizable wad of bills to the doctor

But I have insurance.

Opening her mouth to protest, Donna breathed in the odor of the quiche from the styrofoam container in Brock's hand, the medley of egg, spinach, and berries catching in her throat.

"Thanks man," Brock said. "I can get 'em, but I can't do this myself."

"Hey, we're a great team," the doctor said. "And I'm diggin' the extra income."

"Me too," Brock said a laugh in his voice as he nodded to his head at Donna. "Insurance is gold, right my dear? That, and daddy's money."

What?

"Okay Donna, can you tilt your head back? Let's dilate your pupils."

Plip in one eye then the other. The drops were cool and refreshing in contrast to her soaring temperature. Her vision blurred, a kaleidoscope of dark and glimmering, Brock's face distorting, the doctor…

"This one is very beautiful, Brock."

This one.

"Did you know, my dear Belladonna, in Italy women used belladonna berry juice to dilate their pupils, mimicking the look of arousal to increase their sexual appeal."

Belladonna.

"We use Atropine, which is what we call Belladonna now, in small amounts," he said, wiping a tear from under her eye, "to dilate the pupils for examination. It's not unusual for an ophthalmologist to have large quantities on hand."

Oh God. Could it be?

Her stomach gurgled, a loud protest.

"Consumed in larger amounts, say, in a quiche recipe downstairs…"

I'm an idiot.

These are the Bride Killers.

Sliding from the chair, she writhed on the hard floor, the stench of that quiche filling her brain, her whole body, threading through her bloodstream like hungry tendrils.

"Goodnight, sweet Belladonna."

With Brock's laughter as a requiem, the shade of night engulfed her.

COME HOME

F**ADE IN:**

EXT. TROPICAL BEACH-NIGHT

ANNE is laying on a beach towel, sunglasses on, snoring softly. She is a beautiful woman with long, red hair, gentle curves, and porcelain-like skin.

Though it's dark, the beach is busy with people strolling, drinking, or playing sports in the sand.

. . .

A **DOG** is running down the beach chasing a ball and kicks sand over Anne on the way by.

Anne sputters, wipes the sand from her face, and sits up abruptly.

ANNE
Oh shit!

Anne looks up at the sky then down the beach at all the people. There is no one else laying on the sand or swimming in the water because now it is night.

Frantic, Anne lurches to her feet and examines her body, feeling her stomach and chest, and visually examining her arms and legs.

A **WOMAN** is jogging up the beach. She stops when she reaches Anne.

WOMAN

Um, are you all right?

ANNE
What time is it?

WOMAN
I'm not sure.

ANNE
(Yelling)
I need to know how long I was asleep! I only had four hours!

The woman raises a brow then continues jogging.

Anne starts crying, her breath heavy and panicked. She looks around the beach, counting the people.

ANNE
There's so many. Too many.

. . .

Anne takes off running toward a row of beach cottages.

A **MAN AND WOMAN** are standing on the beach kissing.

ANNE
(Breathless, yelling as she passes the couple)
Get out of here!

The man and woman look at her, heads tilted in confusion.

ANNE (CONT.)
Just go! It's not safe here, if I...

Anne's behavior has drawn the attention of a handful on onlookers. Anne notices and waves her arms at them as she runs.

ANNE

Please! Get away from here!

Anne keeps running until she comes to a quaint little beach cottage with a white picket fence. She bursts through the gate, leaps up the front steps, and flies through the door.

INT. BEACH COTTAGE/KITCHEN-NIGHT

Once inside, Anne locks the door behind her and releases a heavy sigh. She hurries to the kitchen counter, reaches for a fruit bowl, but stops suddenly.

With renewed panic, Anne overturns the fruit bowl, scattering apples and oranges over the counter and floor.

We hear a rustling from somewhere in the cottage.

Anne grabs a knife from the butcher block. As she

does, her hand jerks, sending the knife block crashing to the floor.

INT. BEACH COTTAGE/HALLWAY-NIGHT

Walking down the dark hallway, knife in hand, Anne stops every few steps when one of her limbs jerks awkwardly or her head turns so sharply her neck cracks.

We see light coming from beneath a door at the end of the hall.

Anne creeps to the door, but has to try several times before she can get her hand closed around the knob. Finally, she opens the door.

INT. BEACH COTTAGE/BEDROOM-NIGHT

The bedroom is dark, but we can see the drapes billowing in from a breeze.

· · ·

Anne walks over to shut the window, but she steps on broken glass sprinkled over the carpet. We see the window is broken.

A lamp comes on beside the bed, revealing **ERNEST**, who is sitting on the bed cross-legged. Ernest is naked and covered in kelp. He is holding a banana.

ERNEST
You look quite frazzled, my dear

ANNE
Fuck you. Give it to me.

Ernest maintains eye contact with Anne while peeling the banana.

Anne tries to take a step towards him, but her foot jerks to the side, and she falls to the floor, dropping the knife.

· · ·

ERNEST

(takes a bite of the banana and talks with his mouth full)

Too easy, Anne of the land. Easy to find you, hiding here in this little convenient life...

Ernest takes another bite of the banana and waves the remainder at Anne.

ERNEST (CONT'D)

... in this convenient skin.

Anne pulls herself to a seated position and flexes her hands.

Ernest finishes the banana and tosses the peel out the broken window as he stands from the bed.

Ernest picks the knife off the floor, walks towards Anne, and kneels down in front of her.

. . .

Anne's body convulses. Her arms and legs are kicking and hitting out at the air, her eyes are darting around independently of each other, and her head is twitching in jarring motions.

ERNEST (CONT'D)

If I were you, darling, I might keep more bananas handy, being as they're the only thing that can stop...

Ernest motions the knife over Anne's contorting body.

ERNEST (CONT'D)

... this.

Ernest brings the blade to Anne's throat, then leans in and kisses her on the forehead.

ERNEST

Come back to me, my beautiful wife. You are an ethereal creature. Why must you keep trying to be something else?

· · ·

Anne puts her hand on Ernest's cheek, pressing hard to steady her tremors.

ANNE

We hurt people. Murder them.

ERNEST

Food, my love. Only food.

ANNE

They are human. Beautiful, intelligent, warm.

Anne gulps in air and grasps her chest.

ERNEST

Don't fight it, my Queen. You need the water to breathe. Change back. Come home.

Anne looks right into Ernest's eyes and steadies her hand on his jaw.

. . .

ANNE

No. I will not be that beast anymore.

The flesh on Anne's forearm explodes, and a tentacle sprouts out, impaling Ernest through his jaw and into his brain. Dark blue blood spurts out on the floor.

ANNE (CONT'D)

You'll never get me to go back. They'll all stay safe, and I can live amongst them, where I belong.

A sob and a gargle escape Ernest's throat before he crumples to a lifeless heap on the floor.

Anne scrambles on her hands and knees to a bedside table. Her skin sloughs off as she moves across the hardwood floor, revealing iridescent tentacle suckers pulsating below her flesh.

When she reaches the bedside table, she pulls a banana from the top drawer and devours it, peel and all.

· · ·

The jerking movements cease within minutes, and her skin regenerates, covering the bare patches and sealing the gash left by the escaped tentacle.

Anne stands and goes to the window. She looks out at the beach where a handful of people are strolling along the water with loved ones, jogging, riding bikes, or sitting in the sand looking up at the stars.

Anne smiles, and a silver-red twinkle flashes over her eyes.

FADE OUT.

DECISIONS, DECISIONS

She picked up the tube of Bonnie Bell Root-Beer flavoured lip-gloss. It would set her back two-fifty. All she had was three dollars, but she'd heard Tammy tell Cindy that all the boys liked its taste. She put it back. She could get five Hot Wheels cars for that price.

ETUDE TO STRENGTH

Like wielding the weight of Mjölnir, Alice drew breath into her belly and lifted the word to the sky before bringing it down upon on his hubris and unfounded entitlement.

The word coursed through her veins and exploded from her mouth, a song of power in a single note.

"No."

TOAST AT A FUNERAL

Sera sipped through her smile; each bubble was a memory.

Pop.

Small fingernails caked in Playdoh.

Pop.

Glittering veil blowing in a tropical breeze.

Pop.

Tears and blood, the glorious pain of birth.

Pop.

Wings of death sprouted from her back, her final champagne clutched in a fading hand.

Cheers.

"Oh no fucking way am I taking that table, Tammi." Davida Barker shook her head as she shoved pink artificial sweetener packets into the sugar caddies. Her tables were clean and stocked. She was ready to cash out.

"Come on Davi," Tammi pleaded. "I gotta meet Steve downtown. It's his birthday."

"Tough shit. I got to pick up the kid from my mom's and she's already texted me ten times. Get Rick to take it."

"Rick already bounced. Please Davi? I'll give you ten to take it."

Davi looked over at the table the hostess had just sat. It wasn't her section, and it wasn't even her turn in the rotation, but she had a terrible feeling she was going to have to wait on the table, anyway. It was five till eleven and the kitchen was breaking down, but the rules said they were open until eleven so even at 10:55, if people walked in, they were served. Davi would have been in favor of Cyndi, the idiot hostess, flipping the CLOSED sign early, but that girl was notoriously slow, and the couple walked in and asked for a booth before anybody could pretend the Applebee's was closed.

Davi had drawn a close shift, which was great because she needed the cash and bad because her mom's patience where babysitting was concerned was limited. She had to be at work at six in the morning and when Davi closed, she couldn't pick the kid up until midnight at least. She'd been lucky tonight, and she'd done her closing work quickly. She was almost home-free. Until the table was sat and Tammi decided she was more interested in banging her boyfriend Steve down at the nasty sports bar than in working the last table.

Davi didn't like Tammi. Tammi stole money and took tables that weren't hers, so it was ironic that she was trying to pawn one off on Davi. A glance at the couple seated at booth twenty-three and Davi knew why. The guy was skinny and greasy with a patchy beard and mustache and long hair tucked back under a dirty backward baseball cap. He wore a ratty Pantera t-shirt and dirty jeans that looked like they could stand of their own accord. His companion was an anorexic looking woman of indeterminate age, but she had a distinctivenate look that Davi had named Oxy-Whore. She was painfully thin with her arm bones and sternum clearly visible under sallow, stretched skin. Her dirty blonde hair was thin and pulled back in a tight pony tail that accentuated her frailty. She had dark circles under her eyes, and they were glassy and far-away looking. She barely kept upright at the table.

"Fuck me," Davi sighed. "Twenty bucks, plus you do all my closing work tomorrow."

"Done. I'll give you the twenty tomorrow."

"Fuck you, Tammi. Give me it now or I bail." Davi held out her hand. She knew better than to trust Tammi to be good for anything other than blowing Steve in the shitter at the Front Row.

Tammi scowled and rummaged around in her apron. She pulled out a wad of cash and peeled off a twenty-dollar bill, then threw it down on the table. "You're kind of a cunt, Davi."

"Yeah, well, I ain't a dumb cunt." Davi smiled as she picked up the money and pocketed it. She grabbed some napkins and headed over to the booth. It was worse than she thought. They smelled like cat piss, and when the man grinned, he was missing several teeth. Davi remembered reading once in an anthropology book that loss of dentition in primates was a sign of higher evolution. That textbook writer had never been to Fulton County where meth and oxytocin addictions accounted for major losses of teeth and significant de-evolution of the species.

"Evening. My name's Davi and I'll be taking care of you. Can I get you folks something to drink?" She slapped the beverage napkins down in front of them.

"Big Bud, one of them tall fuckers," the man said. He stared at Davi's tits.

She nodded at him then looked to the woman. "And for you ma'am?"

"Just water for her," the man said as he continued to stare at Davi's chest and grin.

"Sure," Davi said as she headed to the bar to pour his beer. When she got back to the table, she set the drinks down in front of them, and the man immediately started chugging the tall draft beer. He drained it three-quarters of the way before he came up for air, belched, and wiped his lip with his sleeve.

"Whew. I was thirsty," he yelled, then laughed.

"Yep," Davi nodded. "Looks like it. You folks decide on what you want to eat?"

"Yeah, give me a steak."

Davi didn't bother to write it down. She knew how it was going to be cooked.

"And how do you want it cooked?" she asked.

"Well done. Give me double fries. Don't want no faggy salad or shit."

"Sure thing. What can I get for you ma'am?" Davi turned to the woman.

The woman was looking over the menu slowly, turning the sticky pages. She raised her head and looked in Davi's general direction, but her eyes didn't focus on anything. "Chicken fingers," she managed to slowly croak out.

"Yes Ma'am," Davi nodded.

"The small ones," the man said as he finished his beer. "She don't eat much. Bring lots of ranch and ketchup." He held up the empty beer glass and shook it in Davi's face. "More of these, too."

Davi took the glass. "Yes sir."

She chucked the empty glass into the bar sink and rang the food order into the computer. She grinned when she heard the cussing start in the kitchen and knew they had seen it come through. She deposited another beer for the man and headed into the kitchen.

"What the fuck is this shit, Davi? I already closed the grill." Justin, the douchey grill guy slammed things around on the grill in protest.

"What the fuck does it look like? It's a fucking order," Davi said.

"Well tell 'em we're closed." Justin threw his tongs down on his station.

"We ain't closed until eleven, and it wasn't eleven when dipshit sat 'em," Davi said. "So, get busy burning the shit out of his steak."

"This is fucked up. I was already closed."

"Yeah, well, I ain't thrilled about it either." Davi went behind the counter and dropped the fries and chicken fingers in the fryer herself. Billy the Fry Side guy was nowhere to be seen, and she knew he was most likely smoking weed with the kitchen manager out by the dumpster. She ignored Justin's bitching and finished the food. When she delivered it to the table, the man had drained the second beer, and the woman had fallen asleep at the table.

"Fuckin' about time. What'd you have to do, kill the cow?" He slammed the beer glass down for emphasis and then dug into his over-cooked meat, which was a steaming slab of tough grey matter. "Ketchup," he said.

Davi reached over, grabbed it from the table, and set it in front of him. The woman didn't wake up for her chicken tenders and ranch dressing. "Would you like another beer or something else to drink?"

"Another Bud and a shot of Jack," he said around a mouthful of fries and meat. "What kind of name is Davi?" he asked when she came back with his drinks.

"It's short for Davida."

He laughed out loud after he downed the shot.

"Davida's a fat girl's name." He took a long drink of the beer as he leered at her. "You ain't fat."

"Well, thanks, I guess," she said, not knowing exactly what to say that didn't involve the words fuck and off. "You guys want anything else?" She didn't give them much chance to answer as she put the check face-down on the table. "Ok, well, I'll be your cashier whenever you're ready. No rush." She walked off and down the two stairs that led into the bar area to finish cleaning.

Davi had finished all the tables in the bar area and turned around to check on them when she found herself face-to face with the man. The woman was standing by the door, weaving back and forth. The man grinned at Davi and he had something behind his back. "Umm, ready to pay—" Davi stopped talking when he shoved the handgun into her chest.

"I want your cash. All of it in that apron," he said.

Davi's heart thundered in her chest and she felt prickly all over. Her hands shook as she untied her apron and held it up. He took it and grinned. "You the only one here?"

"Yep. Only one with cash, so just go on and let us be," she said.

"What about that register?" he asked as he nodded to the bar.

"Nope. Manager already took the drawer," Davi said.

"Well, guess there ain't nothing else to do here," he said. He smiled meanly at her. She thought his face looked like a rat then. All thin and beady and nasty. "'Cept this."

The noise didn't seem like a gunshot to her. It just seemed like a loud whoosh sound, then she was flat on her back in the bar area and she couldn't breathe. Her chest was heavy and burning and she could smell a funny smell, gunpowder and burnt hair as she lay there. She felt like something was stuck in her throat and she struggled to clear it. When she did, she spit out a big bubble of blood. She tried to move her arms, but they wouldn't move; they felt incredibly heavy, like they were suddenly made of lead. It registered then that he had shot her in the chest, and she began to panic. Her mind raced but she still couldn't move. She thought about the kid sleeping on her mom's old sofa, waiting for her to pick him up, and how she was really going to be late now. She waited and thought she would black out, but she never did. Instead, the prickly feeling got stronger, then it began to radiate throughout her body. She was still, not moving at all, and she didn't even think she was breathing. She couldn't hear anything, but she could still see. Then her body started to tingle, like the whole thing had been a giant sleeping limb, and the sounds all rushed back to her ears. She sucked in a huge lung-full of air then sat up and screamed.

She looked down at her chest. There was a big burnt hole in her shirt. Her skin was raw and angry-red looking, but it was whole and intact, even though she was covered in blood. She ran her hands over it. Everything was still there, just tender, and bloody, her sternum, her guts, her tits. She got to her feet shakily, and when she stood fully upright, the man was still standing there with the gun, staring at her, his toothless mouth gaping. He clutched her apron and the gun. He dropped the gun but not her money, then ran from the restaurant.

Davi didn't follow. Instead, she stood there staring at the gun—which was quite real—as her mind wrapped around the fact that she'd just been shot point-blank in the chest and somehow, she was still breathing without a scratch on her.

A tattered froth of gossamer, the ivory dress flowed in ribbons as Zelda spun the doll in circles, singing, her tiny voice like a blade on crystal.

"On the eve she comes
'Round and 'round
Spinning, swinging
Below the ground—"

"Zelda!"

Willow looked up from her drawing and clucked her tongue. Oh, how Zelda hated when her sister scolded her—she had no business wagging fingers or clucking tongues. Zelda was a moment older, so she should be the one doling out the scoldings.

"I's just singing," Zelda said, hugging the doll to her chest.

"I know," Willow said, returning to her drawing. "You know how Mother hates that song, though."

"Perhaps Father shouldn't have taught us then."

Zelda twirled the doll's indigo tresses through her fingers, humming the song quietly in her throat.

"Still hear you."

"Nuh uh."

"I do!"

Zelda furrowed her brow into an angry caterpillar and plunked down on the floor next to Willow.

"Whatcha drawin'?"

"The woods."

The paper was a palette of browns and spruce, a tangled mass of branches and weeds and tiny yellow eyes peering from hidden holes in the white spaces of the page. Zelda stared, admiring her sister's creation, then rose and walked to the window.

It was a beautiful dusk on their little corner of the world. Their large estate was perched on the cliffs of the Haida Gwaii, overlooking the salt waters of the Pacific and the forest of the mainland. The scene was a painting, pink sky over black water, the moon dancing on the ripples set in motion by fish and insects. A conversation of light flickered between the clouds, the first whisper of storms in the near distance. But another rumble rose with the moon.

"Did mama call us for dinner?" Zelda asked, clutching her grumbling stomach.

"Didn't hear her."

Zelda glanced at the moon, a glowing helium-filled orb now midway up the darkening sky.

"It's late. Why didn't she call us? I'm hungry."

Willow sighed and set her pencil crayon down on her paper.

"Fine. Let's go see if dinner's ready."

Still clutching her doll against her chest, Zelda laced fingers with her sister and walked out of the bedroom. The house was awfully quiet, which was unusual for the hour. At the time when the moon was up and the sun dipped below the ocean, pans would have been clanking against pots and ladles, Mother's wine-filled speech regaling tales of the day to Father who would chortle over a snifter of brandy. And music. Mother would always have music crackling out of the turntable, a mash of folk tunes from distant lands. There was music softly singing in the distance, but harmonic and calculated. Opera, or classical, maybe?

"What is that? Mother never plays that."

The sisters' footsteps fell heavy on the hardwood floors of the upstairs hallway, booming to the levels below. Their steps slowed as they moved farther from their bedroom, the darkness of the hallway swallowing them as they approached the stairs. Zelda's eyes sought the sconces on the wall, usually lit but this night neglected.

"Mother and Father have the lights off still," Zelda said. Her voice was lower. She didn't know why.

Willow must have felt something, too. She slowed and tugged Zelda's hand softly, pulling her behind. Ever the protector, Willow stepped first into the mouth of the stairs, crouching low and peering through the bannisters. Zelda opened her mouth to speak, but Willow raised a hand to maintain the silence.

They waited, listened, barely breathed.

In unison, "Something…"

Willow finished the thought. "Something's not quite right."

Indeed, everything was off. The music, the darkness, the lateness of dinner; Mother and Father were never tardy or neglectful of these very basic functions of home. Fear gargled above the hunger in Zelda's belly, rising like a stone into her throat. And Willow felt it, too. Zelda knew. She knew because what Willow felt, she felt, and Zelda could feel both their hearts beating wild and silent against their ribs and in their temples.

"Can't very well do this for long," Willow said, rising to her feet.

Before Willow chose an action, Zelda lead the way, calling down the stairs, "Mother! Father! You there?"

The words cut through the stagnant air, resonating

on every surface, louder than they had ever been before. The sisters waited, hopelessly willing a response from either parent, but were greeted by a third familiar yet surprising voice.

"Zelda? Willow?"

Isadora, their big sister, called from the front of the house. Her voice was sing-song and aloof, an indication of nothing awry. Tensions melted off the little sisters, unclenching its talons from their throats and bellies.

"I was about to call dinner! Come on down, girls! Table's set and awaits!"

The sisters looked at each other, and the talons struck again, roiling bellies and squeezing throats.

Isadora never called for dinner.

Mother or Father always called for dinner.

Zelda didn't like it, not one little bit.

She had never cared much for Isadora. Isadora was four years her and Willow's senior, but acted thrice that, bossing them like an understudy mother. Mostly, she and Willow had been told—on numerous occasions by both parents, or aunts, uncles, cousins, and the like—that their disdain for Isadora had more to do with their jealously of her prowess and maturity than her dominance. But Zelda knew better. Isadora was a stuck-up ninny who was jealous of her and Willow. They had each other from straight in the womb, and who did Isadora have? Herself and her ego. Willow had a quiet dislike of Isadora, but just as sisters should, she loved and trusted her. Zelda did too, she supposed. Perhaps things would be better when they were adults and equal in all eyes.

Regardless of jealousy or trust, disdain or ego, hunger ruled the moment. Zelda was hungry, and dinner was waiting. The strangeness could take its turn to wait while food was devoured.

Side-by-side, the twins descended the stairs, their eyes drawn to the flickering of candlelight from the dining room at the back of the house. It was faint, but the rest of the main floor was shrouded in darkness, a sight they were unaccustomed to. Usually the main floor was awash with colour and warmth and light, the many bulbs in intricate sconces lighting every corner of the old mansion. Though the walls were papered in dark burgundy and chocolate filigree, the prevalence of flame lit it like a beacon, showcasing every oak crown molding and vase and photograph. But not this night. On this night of the strange interruption of normal, the halls and rooms were coated in layers of the black silk of darkness, only shapes and sharp textures revealed by the flame reaching from the end of the long hall.

"Girls!" Isadora called, her lyrical voice coming now from the kitchen adjacent the dining room. "I am preparing your plates, now! Take your seats, if you please!"

Not an inkling of Mother or Father. No voice, no clinking of wine or liquor glass, no properly lit passageways. Willow placed her fingertips against the wallpaper, leading Zelda by the hand towards the light. Though ravenous, Zelda hesitated to follow; several times, Willow had to give her a sharp tug to keep her sister at her hip. As they approached the mouth of the dining room, the kitchen appeared on their left, lit only by a single candle on the stove. Isadora turned to them as they stopped in the entry way. Her face was powered in flour, her arms elbow deep in Mother's floral cooking gloves, Father's ratty, ember-burnt campfire apron hanging loose off her wirey frame.

"It's fish tonight, girls. Your favourite, yes Zelda?

Zelda's mouth filled with saliva, the smell of steaming seafood wafting through the main floor. Fish had been prepared with Mother's special seasoning, a recipe passed down through generation on memory rather than paper. The night might be weird, but there was mama's spice, so nothing else mattered.

"Where's Mother?" Willow asked.

Isadora met Zelda's eye, answering without a blink. "Why, waiting for dinner! For you to join us so we can get started."

Willow jumped in. "But why are you making dinner?"

Hands on hips, Isadora pursed her lips into a pout. "I can cook just fine. Mother entrusted me to this fine Friday meal, and I was excited for the challenge. I've had my first blood, I'll have you know. It's time for me to practice running a home."

The twins looked at each other, then back at Isadora. No one was smiling.

"Look, it's food. If you don't fancy it, there will be something else. You needn't worry though. It's edible."

It does smell amazing, Zelda thought, eyeing the fish on the carving tray.

Hesitantly content with the odd changing of the guard, the sisters left Isadora to her preparations and continued to the dining room at the end of the hall.

The dining room was bright, dozens of iron sconces on the walls lit with vigorous flame, the colours and textures of the room vibrant, dancing with the moving flames. The table was set as it should be, all cutlery in its place, napkins folded like trumpeter swans just like Mother did on special occasions. All expected side dishes were laid across the table, a bounty of yams and peas and rolls ready to swim in pools of gravy. Most importantly, Mother and Father were there, each seated at the ends of the table.

But all was not as it should be.

And the twins were no longer content with the new routine.

"Isn't this lovely?" Isadora cooed, swooping into the dining room, silver platter in hand. "A right proper feast, this is."

The sound of the platter being set on the table, though gentle, rattled like cymbals in Zelda's brain, loosening tears that poured down her face.

"Isadora."

It was the only word Willow could manage, which was more than Zelda, who couldn't manage to choke out a single syllable. Her breath disappeared, the wind knocked out of her by shock, the only voice her own screaming in her own brain.

What have you done?

"Now girls, sit down. You're already tardy for dinner, but thankfully so was I. The food's still hot, so——"

Isadora's explanation was cut off by Willow's shrill scream, loud and pained enough to strain the crystal goblets at each place setting. Willow tentatively approached Mother, snot and tears running down her face, incoherent ramblings exploding out of her mouth.

Zelda stayed quiet and stared.

Stared at her Mother's throat open, blood and vomit spilled over the front of her smock.

Zelda stared at her father, gardening tool hilt deep in one ear, poking out the other.

The ivory table cloth—the one with the delicate little flowers Mother had embroidered herself by hand; oh how proud she was of that table cloth—now saturated with a crimson sheen, the life of both parents marring its purity.

"What-ever do you mean?" Isadora said, shrugging her shoulders.

Willow sputtered, "How could you... why did you..."

Isadora waved a hand dismissively. "You wouldn't understand, the two of you. Maybe one day, when you're older and wiser like me."

Isadora grabbed the carbines of water from the liquor cart and started filling the goblets. Willow continued sputtering and Zelda continued staring as she served up a single plate of dinner. When she was done, she walked over to the window and looked out at the ocean, hands behind her back.

"They were going to sell this place, you know. Our home. Can you imagine? There's nothing quite like this place, out here on the ocean all by itself. We are one with the woods and the sea here—"

She didn't get a chance to finish. Willow launched at her, catching her by surprise. With fist-fulls of Isadora's hair, Willow thrashed and tore, ripping out great red curls and clawing at her face. But Isadora was older and stronger, and very quickly restrained Willow.

"You monster!" Willow spat, kicking and biting at the air in hopes of taking a piece—any piece—of her sister.

"Perhaps," Isadora said, "but this is my home. And now it really is. *My* home."

With her arms wrenched behind her back, Willow was forced out onto the patio and down into the back-yard. Zelda followed, taking care not to move too close lest her older sister grab her, too.

"Mama," Zelda said, weeping quietly. "Mama, help us Mama."

Mother couldn't hear. Neither could father. But Isadora did. And she laughed, a deep and demented chortle from deep in her belly.

"Ah, wee Zelda, ever the fool. Your flights of fancy won't carry you away on their wings this time, my naive little dear. Mommy and Daddy are gone, and this," Isadora swept a hand around her, motioning to the property, "is my world now."

Willow cried out in anger and protest, struggling violently against Isadora's tight grasp.

What could she do? She wouldn't dare—

But she did dare. Isadora let go, and Willow stood, freed and stunned for but a moment before launching back at her older sister with reignited fury. It didn't last long. Their bodies collided with an audible squelch, then both girls fell still and silent. Willow took a step back, too slow for Zelda's comfort, and her hands worked their way to her own belly where they wrapped around the hilt of the fillet knife stuck in her abdomen.

Zelda found her voice.

"Willow? Willow… no… Mama…"

Willow dropped to the ground, bloody drool sputtering from her lips. She clawed at her stomach, her hands slipping off the gore-soaked blade until her eyes widened and she crumpled into the grass. Zelda felt like she was floating as she walked to her sister's side, kneeling beside her in the soft ground.

"Willow, you're so pale."

She stroked her raven-black hair, smoothing it across the grass. Everything looked midnight blue in the moonlight—Willow's hair, the shimmering grass, the fur…

A meaty hand grabbed Zelda's arm and hauled her off the ground just before the wolf pounced, sinking its teeth into Willow's throat and tearing out a chunk. They locked eyes, Zelda and the Wolf, as Willow's meat dripped off its lips. It nuzzled its snout into the nape of Willow's neck and clamped its jaws around her neck to get a firm grip. Then slowly, maintaining eye contact with Zelda, backed into the woods, dragging Willow with it. Zelda watched until the soles of Willow's pink feet disappeared into the harsh, mangled brush.

"Willow."

"Come now," Isadora said, hand on Zelda's back, guiding her across the grass.

"No, Willow. Come back."

Zelda's voice was below a whisper, audible to only her mind's ears, but she kept breathing the words, watching the tree line for her sister, even as it moved farther and farther away. By the time they reached the water, Isadora was carrying her, traversing the rocky shore and submerging them both in the cold water of the Pacific.

The frigid cold stole Zelda's breath as Isadora pushed her under the water. The waves lapped peacefully against the shore, a cathartic rhythm that moved with the floating gossamer of the dress on the doll clutched to Zelda's chest. Zelda held that doll tight, willing it to bring air to her lungs, to be her mother, her sister, anyone that would still be alive and love her and save her from her watery grave…

WHO WROTE WHAT

- THE LESSON by Jessica Raney
- CREATED BY YOU by Jae Mazer
- HIGHER LEARNING by Jessica Raney
- SHE GREW WINGS by Jae Mazer
- BEST SERVED COLD by Jessica Raney
- HENRY'S A DICK by Jae Mazer
- DESTINY RIDES A POLE by Jessica Raney
- PRECISELY by Jessica Raney
- TRUE NORTH by Jae Mazer
- WAITING FOR TAMMY ALBRECHT by Jessica Raney
- CLOSE ENOUGH by Jae Mazer
- SURE WAS by Jessica Raney
- LUKA'S DESERT SCI-FI MOVIE by Jessica Raney

- COTTON LOVE by Jae Mazer
- HOW MAGGIE GOT HER GROOVE BACK by Jessica Raney
- THE DOWNFALL OF WINNIFRED BEISSNER by Jae Mazer
- THE LAST NINE SECONDS by Jessica Raney
- LUCKY #48 by Jae Mazer
- SHOW OF POWER by Jae Mazer
- CHECKPOINT FIVE by Jessica Raney
- HE'S MINE by Jessica Raney
- PLEASE by Jae Mazer
- THE SHADE OF NIGHT by Jae Mazer
- COME HOME by Jae Mazer
- DECISIONS, DECISIONS by Jessica Raney
- ETUDE TO STRENGTH by Jae Mazer
- TOAST AT A FUNERAL by Jae Mazer

ACKNOWLEDGMENTS

Acknowledgements

Lots of people help with these things. First, thanks to the great people at NYC Midnight for always accepting my fifty bucks. I can waste money like nobody's business and this way is one of my favorites that doesn't involve vodka or grab bags. NYC Midnight has made me a better writer.

Thanks to all my critique group peoples, especially Amber. You are always up to read stuff and your critiques are always thoughtful and helpful. You have made me a better writer.

And, of course, thanks to Jae. When we started

meeting at Dennys, I thought cool, I'm going to get a ton of writing done. If that were all I got, I would still be lucky. As it turns out, I got way more. You challenge me. You are the best person to talk writing and everything else with. You are generous and kind. Wicked smart and funny. I'm impressed by your talent and skill and how hard you work. I think the most fortunate day of my life is the day we met. You make me a better writer and a better person. I'm proud of this work and I'm even more proud that I got to do it with you. I hope that in 20 years, when I'm still 39, we'll still have an LDM agenda. Thank you for sharing with me. I corn you.

Jess

ACKNOWLEDGMENTS

I would like to thank coffee, wine, vodka, super blood wolf moons, and Jess.

Jae

ABOUT THE AUTHOR

Jessica Raney is an author of speculative fiction. She has two collections of short stories: *Oddballs: A Collection of Short Fiction* and *Dreadful Pennies: A Collection of Short Things*. Her first full length novel, Tooth and Nail, was released in 2018. Her work has also appeared in the anthology, *Hair Raising Tales of Horror*. When not navigating Houston traffic or writing, she's dealing with her cat/dog/demon/baby, Gimli.

ALSO BY JESSICA RANEY

Oddballs

Dreadful Pennies

Tooth and Nail

These Violent Delights

ABOUT THE AUTHOR

Jae Mazer is a Canadian who was born in Victoria, British Columbia, and grew up in the prairies of Northern Alberta. After spending the majority of her life battling sasquatches in the Great White North, she migrated south to Texas to have a go at the armadillos. Now she enjoys life as a mom, a musician, and a connoisseur and creator of horror, science fiction, and fantasy. Many moons ago, a rampant love of reading led her to believe she could weave a good tale herself, and she now has seven novels under her belt, as well as short stories published in various anthologies.

ALSO BY JAE MAZER

Landing in Eden

Delivery

Pal Tailor

Gahl's Door

Chrysalis and Clan

Crone

Beautiful Beasts

Also written by Jae, under the Pen Name J.M. Adler

Notch

Co-Authored with Gerry Mazer

Ripples of Silence

Jae Mazer has short stories included in the following
anthologies:

Eclectically Heroic, by Inklings Publishing

Hair Raising Tales of Villainous Confessions, by Mad
Girl's Publishing